WALKING
Into A Nightmare

WALKING
Into A Nightmare

RHONDA RUSSELL

TATE PUBLISHING
AND ENTERPRISES, LLC

Published by Tate Publishing & Enterprises, LLC
127 E. Trade Center Terrace | Mustang, Oklahoma 73064 USA
1.888.361.9473 | www.tatepublishing.com

Tate Publishing is committed to excellence in the publishing industry. The company reflects the philosophy established by the founders, based on Psalm 68:11,
"The Lord gave the word and great was the company of those who published it."

Book design copyright © 2015 by Tate Publishing, LLC. All rights reserved.
Cover design by Samson Lim
Interior design by Gram Telen

Published in the United States of America

ISBN: 978-1-68142-295-4
1. Fiction / General
2. Fiction / Thrillers / Crime
15.06.17

This book is dedicated to women who are starting to make their way in life alone.

ACKNOWLEDGMENTS

Huge thank-yous go out to Kandi Post for her assistance, time, and knowledge in all she does for the success of my books.

PREFACE

The author has been led to write this drama novel from personal reference to drama that occurs in our world today. Drama, being one of the most fascinating features of entertainment, plays a mystery in everyone's life accidentally or intentionally. Although this book is truly a combination of fictional thoughts, it is something to ponder on. I have also written the I Promise You the Moon trilogy.

CHAPTER 1

On this warm, bright, sunny morning in the late month of May, the sun, smiling its friendly warmth and brightness through Jan's bedroom window, was calling attention to every plant and flower in its path to arise to the gleaming light. Jan yawned and started waking to the brightness. Coming to the reality of her day's planned events, she became giddy and excited. She had just completed her college years, and today she was starting to reach out to make her dream future a reality.

She arose and started her morning routine of dressing and made her way to the kitchen, where her father and mother sat at the table.

"Good morning, young lady." Her mother smiled, even though she felt some sadness. Her baby was moving today, leaving the house, the town, and the state.

"Are you ready for today?" asked her dad.

"Oh! I am so excited. I feel like I am just jumping inside. I know this will be great!" Jan answered.

Jan sat down to eat a light breakfast and have coffee with her parents. She realized it was going to be hard on them.

Jan Williams had graduated with honors from the college in her town, so she had been able to remain at home. Her parents had hoped she could find a position in their small town of Berkley, Nebraska, so she wouldn't have to leave home just yet.

Before her graduation day, she had been accepted for a designing position in Callaway, Iowa, a place none of them had ever heard of before. It was a long way from home, but it would be a new start for Jan.

Finishing breakfast, she returned to her room and started packing up. She could remember back when her parents bought this house, the first time she saw her room, how excited she was at only five, and now leaving the safety and security of this room, she was anxious and excited. This was her chance to scope out the outside world and make new friends.

It took most of the morning to pack up her room. Her parents helped as much as they could, even though they just wanted to beg her to stay. Jan was twenty now and had every right to leave the nest.

They had driven to Callaway two weeks before and found an apartment for her. The city was so big, and Jan's parents were afraid for her. They met some of the people in the firm of Jones and Keller Designs for Today. Everyone was nice, and they hoped Jan would make friends soon.

Jan loaded her car and a small trailer with the belongings she would be starting her life with. As she looked at her empty room, there sat Mr. Tuttles, the large panda her dad had given her many years ago. He was her favorite, and Mr. Tuttles had to move with Jan.

Her mother had prepared a nice lunch for them as she knew it would be the last meal they would share together for a while. Her father gave the blessing for the meal with tears burning his eyes. He politely asked, "Jan, do you have everything you need? We can round up whatever it is, and you can leave tomorrow!"

"Dad, it won't be any easier tomorrow or next week than it is today. I have everything I need. Besides, I will be home again." Laughing, she added, "Mr. Tuttles and I, we will be back!"

Ken and Corene Williams had wanted several children, and after many years of not successfully having any children, when Jan came, it was the happiest moments and years of their lives. They had grown to be so superprotective of her, and they both knew it was time to let her go.

Her mother, Corene, looked at Jan with tears running down her face. "Jan, honey, it is so hard on us to see you leave home. We both know you have to do what is right for you. It is just so difficult for us to accept. We are not trying to make it harder on you."

"I know, Mom, but you should be proud. You both have loved me so much, and you've done a good job raising me. I plan to use all this in my new life."

"Your academic years and the work you did in the church, it just won't be the same."

"I'll miss everyone, but I'll be back. There are always vacations and holidays."

When lunch was finished, Jan completed her loading the trailer and cleaning up what had been her room, her solitude for many years. She realized it was going to be hard on her as well.

The last box was loaded, and it was time for Jan to head to Callaway. Her parents stood, trying to be brave and not act difficult.

Her father, choking back the tears, said, "I want you to call when you stop for the night so we know everything is okay. Be sure and pay attention to your gauges and how the car is running. Call if you have any problems."

"Yes, Dad, I will. If I don't go now, I'll never make it even halfway today." She laughed to lighten the sad mood her parents were in.

As she got in her car and drove down the street, she could see her parents waving to her, and the tears were rolling like raindrops. She took time to say a prayer to start her trip. "Thank you, Jesus, for giving me such godly parents to teach and raise me the proper way."

As Jan drove toward her destination, she got hungry and decided to stop in a small town for gas and a snack and then continue on. She felt strange making such a long trip on her own, but she felt all grown up now that she was heading for her new life. As she got back in her car, there sat Mr. Tuttles, her lifelong friend, in the passenger seat.

"I know things will be okay, Mr. Tuttles. We are going to do this together." Down the road she headed.

Several hours had passed. As she drove, she sang to the radio and talked to Mr. Tuttles, who was still in the passenger seat. Things were going quite well. She was excited about the new job and the move.

The sun was starting to dim and go down on the other side of the horizon, and she was almost to the halfway mark. She was getting tired and hungry for a hot meal and a warm bath, and she was sure she could sleep like a baby.

She was thinking about her evening plans when she heard an explosion, like someone had shot a gun. The trailer started weaving and pulling on the car. She immediately pulled over. Getting out of the car, she walked back to her trailer. She had blown a tire. *How strange*, she thought. *Dad checked everything, and there is not that much weight to cause a tire to blow.* She returned to the car to call her dad to send someone from the trailer company to change the tire. She saw a shadow and looked out the passenger window. She saw nothing. As she turned to the driver's window, there stood a man. She jumped and screamed. She rolled down her window, and the man asked, "Looks like you blew a tire. Need some help, little lady?"

"Where did you come from? I just got out and looked at the trailer. There weren't any cars behind me!" She was still shaken.

The man was unclean, with a smell of a mechanic and grease on his clothes. His long hair was tied back, and he had a worn-out ball cap on his head. He hadn't shaved in several days, and quite frankly, Jan was frightened of his appearance.

He walked back to the trailer and found the spare tire. He easily changed the tire on the trailer. Jan continued to watch through the side mirror, not getting out of the car.

When the tire was changed, it was almost dark, not much traffic. He walked back to the driver's window. Jan rolled the window partway down.

"All finished, ma'am. You need to be very careful on these roads," he advised.

Still shaken and upset, she asked, "How much do I owe you for changing the tire?"

"Oh, a few bucks. Whatever you think is fair."

As Jan reached in her purse to get a few dollars to pay the man, she felt a sting on her neck and began to feel dizzy. She turned to look at the man. He was now unlocking her door. She felt defenseless against him.

He scooted her over in the passenger seat next to Mr. Tuttles. He did not say anything, just got into the car and started the engine. The car began to roll forward still pulling the trailer behind. She thought, *I am so sleepy. If I just close my eyes, when I wake up, maybe this will be a dream, and it will be all over.*

CHAPTER 2

Ken and Corene were watching television, and on intervals, they would look at the clock to see what time it was, trying not to let the other know they were concerned. Corene got up and went to the kitchen to prepare supper. For the first time, she was at a loss. She didn't know what to fix nor how much, it being just the two of them. She didn't feel like inviting friends over just now. She busied herself preparing the meal, trying to act as normal as she could, yet tears stung at her eyes. When it was finished and on the table, she caught herself just as she was about to call Jan. She walked to the living room. "Ken, supper's ready and on the table."

"Okay, thank you, sweetie. I am getting a little hungry."

Sitting down at the table, Ken gave the blessing for the meal. He then added, "Lord, be with Jan. We are trying to accept this change. Give us strength to adjust and accept."

As they sat quietly eating, Corene put her hand on Ken's. "I don't know if I can do this. I am trying so hard to be strong, but it's too overwhelming and too much to change at once."

"I know, honey, but we have each other, and we will keep trying every day. It will be okay, you'll see."

They finished dinner in silence, knowing what the other was thinking.

Ken got up and headed for the living room. "Why don't you leave the dishes? Come and join me in the living room. Rest and watch some television. We'll wait for Jan's call together."

"It won't take me long. I need to keep busy. I'll be along shortly." She got up and put the leftovers away and did the dishes, remembering the talks that Jan and she had over the dishes through her high school years. She finished cleaning the kitchen and returned to the living room. They continued looking at the clock. Still no call.

"I think I'll take a hot bath, and that way, after Jan calls, we will be ready for bed," Corene suggested.

"Okay, I will call you if she calls while you are in the tub."

Ken had started to doze off and abruptly woke up wondering if he missed Jan's call. It had been almost an hour. Corene returned to the living room. "Well, I feel better."

"That's good. I dozed off while you were taking your bath."

As they watched television, it got later and later. Corene was getting worried. "Why doesn't she call? She knows how we worry. Surely she would not just forget to call, and she always calls. I hope nothing is wrong."

"Maybe she got to the motel, ate, took a bath, and fell asleep. If she doesn't call by morning, I'll call her. Let's give her a chance tonight. Don't worry, I'm sure she's okay. She would have called if there were any problems."

It just got later and later. Corene was about to burst into tears, just knowing something was wrong. Ken was upset inside, not believing Jan had not called when he'd told her to call when she made it to the motel.

The news came on, and they both listened carefully. Nothing was said about any car wrecks. After the news was over, Ken reached for Corene's hand. "Honey, let's go to bed and try to get some rest. I know it's difficult, but I promise I will call her in the morning."

Once in bed, Corene's mind wandered to all the things that could have happened. *What if she's on the roadside hurt and no one can see* her? Tears came to her eyes as she prayed, "Be with my little girl, and please keep her safe!"

The two dozed, tossing and turning. They walked the floor and fought their fears most of the night. As early morning approached, they went to sleep from pure exhaustion. It had been such a rough night.

They awoke startled as the phone by the bed was ringing. *Oh thank God,* Corene thought, *it's Jan.*

Ken picked up the phone. Corene watched, fighting the urge to grab the phone from him so she could talk to her baby. Then she saw his face drain of all color. He bolted straight up in bed.

"What are you saying? She never arrived at the motel? I'm not worried about the money. I want to know where my daughter is!" Ken listened for a few more minutes, firing questions at whoever was on the other end of the line. After a terse good-bye, he finally hung up.

Corene froze and went limp. She thought she was going to faint. "Ken, what's happened?" Crying hysterically, she said, "I knew something was wrong! What did the motel person say?"

"That was the manager, and she had been there all night and is preparing to get off work. She said Jan never arrived last night. Only a portion of the room charge could be returned to our credit card from the reservation. I told her I didn't care about the money. Just want to know what happened to our daughter."

Both were extremely upset. Corene started screaming and crying. "Oh dear God in heaven, where is my baby? I know she shouldn't have left. Now we've lost her."

"Honey, settle down. I've got to think what to do."

They got dressed and drove to the sheriff's department. The sheriff was a longtime close friend of Ken's. Maybe he could help them since this was now a major emergency.

They entered the department, both very shaken from the phone call they received. Ben Campo had arrived only shortly before the Williamses arrived and was in his office drinking coffee. He saw Ken and Corene and was very surprised to see them, yet he could tell by their demeanor something was terribly wrong. Ben got up and went out to meet them.

"What brings you two here so early in the morning?"

"It's Jan, Ben. We need your help!" Ken exclaimed. Corene was crying and becoming white, completely beside herself; she was becoming completely out of control.

"Come into my office and tell me what's going on. Didn't Jan leave for Callaway yesterday? Have a seat and tell me what's going on. Sue, could you please bring two cups of coffee in for the Williamses?"

Ken proceeded to tell Ben. "She left after lunch yesterday for Burk. That's the halfway point. We made reservations for her motel. The motel manager called just a little while ago. Ben, Jan never arrived in Burk."

"Okay, give me the information on her—the car, the trailer. I have a friend who is on the highway patrol up through that way, and maybe he will make a run up through there to see if there is anything suspicious going on. You folks go home, and as soon as I hear anything, I will be in contact with you."

"Oh, Ben, bless you. Thank you for helping. I knew you would know what to do."

"Just find my baby, Ben. Please find my baby!" Corene was hysterical.

"Corene, I know you are upset. You have to get ahold of yourself. Panic is not going to help anything. We are going to find Jan. Go home, get a bite of breakfast, and I will come by with the first bit of information we find out as soon as I can."

They left Ben's office to get in the car. Ken was holding Corene as close as he could, and he knew he was going to have to be strong for both of them. They drove to the next block to their favorite diner, the Breakfast Delight. As Ken pulled into the parking lot, Corene remarked, "I don't know if I can eat anything or not. I feel so sick to my stomach."

"You need to eat something, even if it is just toast."

They sat at the first empty table just inside the door. The waitress on duty was Cookie Gilespie, a close friend of Jan's.

Cookie stayed here. Why couldn't Jan have stayed? We wouldn't be going through this now, Corene thought as she laid eyes on Cookie.

Cookie approached the table. She was always so happy and jolly. Jan and Cookie had gone out the night before Jan left.

She will be crushed to find out we don't know where Jan is.

"Hi, Dad and Mom, did Jan get off as planned? Boy, I sure am going to miss her."

"Cookie, you had better sit down. We have some news, and it would be best to tell you if you were sitting down. Jan's missing!"

"What do you mean missing?"

"The motel manager called earlier this morning to let us know that Jan never arrived last night. The police are looking for her now." Ken tried to explain gently to Cookie so as not to upset her any more than he had to.

Tears started rolling down her face. "No! This can't be. She has been looking forward to this day for months. We even talked about moving in together in a few months." Cookie took their orders and hurriedly kept busy. She didn't want to show how upset she was. Her jolly personality was dimmer now. She returned to their table, where Ken was holding Corene's hands tightly to give her added strength. Cookie sat down their breakfast order and coffee. "Is there anything I can do to help?"

"No, just pray and keep Jan in your heart. That's all we ask at this point," answered Ken.

"I am so sorry this is happening! Please keep me informed. I am worried about her."

After breakfast, they drove on home. Ken called his boss at the local newspaper and reported the crisis they were going through. "I just can't leave my wife, and Ben told us to wait here at the house."

"I understand, and I would do the same. Let us know if there is anything we can do!"

"Thank you so much for your kindness and understanding. I will keep you informed as soon as I know anything."

Ken hung up the phone. "You know, Corene, there is one thing I didn't even think of. I'm going to call Jan's phone." With high expectations, he dialed Jan's number. The phone rang twice and then shut off. He felt his heart sink, but did not express what his thoughts were.

Corene asked, "Well...did she answer?"

"No, honey, it just rings. I guess her voice mail is full."

Corene went to lie down. She was so exhausted from the long night and lack of sleep, and her mind was racing. "Please wake me when Ben comes."

"You know I will." Ken texted Jan's phone. At least maybe she would know they were looking for her, but it didn't go through. Ken fell in his chair utterly devastated, crying uncontrollably for the first time since they heard Jan was missing. With Corene resting, this was his first chance to finally just let his feelings go. He felt completely helpless. Jan needed him, and there wasn't anything he could do to help her. He could picture her as a baby and the different things she did in her younger years. He closed his eyes and dozed off in a peaceful sleep, seeing Jan smiling at him.

He awoke abruptly to the doorbell ringing. He jumped to answer it, and there stood Ben.

"Come in. Do you have any news on Jan?"

"Some. I don't know if it will give you much hope, but it's a start."

"Let me wake Corene. Have a seat. Can I get you anything to drink?" Ken went off to their room, where Corene lay resting. He hated to wake her when she finally looked so peaceful, but he knew she wanted to hear what Ben had found out. "Honey, Ben is here with some news."

Corene got up groggily. It took her a few seconds to gain some coherence. She was dreaming of Jan and happier days, so she was a little disoriented to what was going on around her.

When the couple walked into the living room a few minutes later, Ben was there with a cup in his hand. "How about some coffee? I took the liberty to make some. I hope you don't mind."

Ignoring Ben's lighthearted comment, Ken demanded, "What have you found out?"

"Sorry," Ben began, "I called my friend, Mike Temple. He was glad to help us. He told me he got about fifty miles outside of Burk, and he found black marks on the highway that appeared to be fresh marks. Let me ask you this, Ken, did you check Jan's car and trailer before she left?"

"They both had new tires all the way around. The car was running in tip-top shape. I checked everything under the hood and the hitch. I checked everything. I wouldn't have let her leave if there were anything wrong," Ken replied.

"I know that, but I had to ask. Mike found a small, slender tire strip nailed to the highway. It looked to him like someone put it there to disable a trailer and not the vehicle itself. He didn't want any more marks on the road than he had to. Mike is going to take dogs out to search, and we are going to search the abandoned farms in the area. It's going to be pretty hard to hide a car and trailer."

"Oh, thank you so much for coming by. It is some hope to lean on."

"You just need to carry on with your lives as normal as you can. I will keep in touch with you as I learn anything."

As Ben walked to the door, he said, "Corene, don't worry. We are going to find your daughter, I promise."

They turned on the television; news flashes were on every channel about Jan's disappearance. It was close to twenty-four hours now. Ken and Corene could only have faith and believe in God that their Jan would be found and brought home safe and sound. The news broadcaster reported that roadblocks were being set up all over the state; search parties, with the help of dogs, were looking all over the area where the black marks were found.

As the hours rolled by, the tension got worse between Ken and Corene. Ken was uncertain how he could keep his strength up, let alone his devastated wife's. He felt weaker by the day. It was now going on two days since Jan went missing; it actually felt like a lifetime.

Corene felt weaker as well. They had always a good marriage. How would they endure if something happened to Jan? Neighbors had started coming by and were helping out as much as possible. They would visit and help with light cleaning around the house, helping Corene with the laundry, and the men gathered to help Ken with the outside chores. Many of the ladies from the church were bringing in meals. Things were running as organized as they could, considering the circumstances. Everyone was concerned about Jan and did what they could to lighten the load for Ken and Corene.

The morning of the third day, as Ken and Corene were eating breakfast, the front doorbell rang. It was Ben. "Ken, they found the car and the trailer. Jan was not with the car, however. It was hidden in an old barn twenty-five miles from the site of the blowout."

It gave them added hope, but where was Jan?

"Can you go with me, and we will go get the car and trailer and bring it back home?"

At that point, Corene burst out, "I want to go!"

"I don't advise it, Corene. I know it's hard staying here, but it's worse out there."

Ben and Ken jumped in the patrol car and drove toward Burk. They stopped where the black marks were, now three days old. The hillsides were covered with police and people with dogs. Stands were set up with water and energy snacks. Sandwiches were being brought out to supply the searchers. Tents were set up, large lights put up, and they were searching in shifts. Roadblocks were set up on every road in and out of the area. A massive search was going on to find out what had taken place here just three days previous.

"Ken, take the car and trailer and go home. Stay with Corene. She needs you. We don't know what we will find now. Just pray, but Corene needs you now."

Ken agreed as this was just too much for even him. As he got into Jan's car, it looked the same as it did the day Jan left. The car had been dusted for fingerprints, and so had the trailer. All that was found were Ken's and Jan's prints. There beside him was Mr. Tuttles, right where Jan had left him, Ken could not control his tears, and he remembered the day he had given the bear to Jan. This is the first time that he had ever been far away from Jan.

Ken arrived home late with the car. Corene ran out to meet him in hopes that Jan was with him. Ken went into the house carrying Mr. Tuttles. They grabbed each other standing in the doorway, sharing their sorrow and empathy and clutching Mr. Tuttles to seek the answers they longed for.

It was very late and now going into the fourth day, they retired for the night with Mr. Tuttles between them as they had done so many times when Jan was a small child. Exhaustion took over, and they fell asleep praying for a miracle to come soon.

The morning sun peered through the windows. They arose with great expectations. They shared small meaningless conversation over breakfast. Ken proceeded to inform Corene of everything Ben was doing to find Jan.

The phone rang, startling them. It was Ben! "Honey, they found the man that kidnapped Jan!"

Corene began to cry. "Did he tell them where she's at?"

"They are questioning him now. We'll pray it won't be long now."

As the day passed, searchers were still looking for Jan. The police went to the man who started this nightmare. Mike called Ben. "One of the roadblocks called. They have an old beat-up wrecker with a grungy-looking man driving stopped. They searched his truck and found a bag with needles and bottles of injectable medications to paralyze the system. They also found small strips to puncture tires. His name is Mark Winters. He roams this country area, scavenging, and sometimes disables cars. We have a clue, though. We asked what he did with Jan. 'Anything that precious and fragile belongs in a treasure box!' was his only response. We figure she is buried somewhere, so we are looking for fresh earth."

Ben told Mike, "I can't go to the family with this. We have to find Jan."

"We will take the dogs and continue to search. We will find her."

The morning of the fifth day, a group of four searchers wandered outside the parameters, unaware of where they were, and the dogs started pulling on them, running faster down a gulch. They could hardly control the dogs, which were barking, howling, sniffing, bouncing, and digging. There by a tree was a large area with no grass. A small shed with a generator was running, and fresh dirt covered the area. All four searchers held their flare guns up and fired, making all the noise they could make to alert the rest of the search parties. With small shovels, they started digging. Much to their surprise, there were hoses leading down though the fresh earth.

As the searchers were digging, more searchers came running and joined in. They hit something hard as they were digging; it was a covering to a grave. Everyone was digging frantically and clearing the fresh earth to see what was beneath the wooden covering.

The door was pried open. There lay a young teenage female with oxygen tubing coming into the wooden grave. She looked frantic and scared. They called the ambulance and continued to dig; there was another young teenage girl, and another. As the last wooden structure was opened, there lay Jan. All four were in shock but alive. Jan had been buried alive for five days; each of the other girls had been buried a day longer, and the first had been buried for ten days. The girls were strong and had maintained their faith and prayed they would be found. Each of them was transferred to the hospital.

Mike called Ben. "We found your girl! She's at the hospital in Burk. She's going to be okay."

"Oh, thank you, Mike. Now that's news I can call the family with!"

Ben got in his car and drove right to the Williamses' home. Ken saw Ben pull up, and he knew this was it. His heart dropped to his feet as he answered the door. Ken and Corene stood holding on to each other.

"We found Jan! She is in the hospital in Burk. She's going to be fine, but she's in shock."

"Where was she? Did he hurt her?"

"Ken, Corene, I don't know any easy way to tell you this. She had been buried alive with three other girls for the past five days."

"Oh my god!" Corene screamed. "I can't imagine what she's been through."

"The two of you go. Go to Burk to see your little girl!"

CHAPTER 3

In Burk, Mark Winters has been taken into the interrogation room by the local authorities to be questioned about the four young women found buried. "I told you they were treasures and belonged in a treasure box. That is all I plan to say. Do whatever you want, but when I get out, I plan on continuing to collect treasures."

"Place this man under arrest and charge him with four counts of kidnapping and four counts of attempted murder."

"I didn't kill anyone. I kept them hydrated with IVs and pain-free."

"I want you to know that you have just admitted to this crime. If I have to watch you the rest of my life, you will never bury another woman! Get him out of my sight!"

Ken and Corene made the trip to Burk, trying to hurry to the hospital; five days had been too long to not know where Jan was. They were happy to know she had been found. A weight had been lifted, yet they needed to see that she was okay.

Ben called Corene on her cell phone to relay the news from the Burk police. "How's your trip, Corene? Are you getting close to the hospital?"

"We are about a couple of hours away. We have been driving straight through. What's going on?"

"I called to let you know the Burk police have arrested Mr. Winters. They got an admission from him about what he was doing. I thought you would want to know he will be prosecuted for this."

"Thank you for calling. It is good to know he will not be able to hurt anyone else. We will be staying in Burk with Jan until she can come home."

On arriving at the Burk County Hospital, the anxiety was mounting. "We are Jan Williams's parents. Where is she?"

"She is in room 538 north. She is quite shaken up. I am so glad you are here. We have all four of the girls in the same room. We have had to have someone stay with them."

"Thank you. We will go right up."

Ken and Corene headed toward the elevator and pushed the button to go to the fifth floor. The elevator doors opened.

Quickly they spotted the signs directing them to the fifth floor north and headed toward 538.

As they walked to the room, security guards were standing at the door. Ken and Corene identified themselves to the guards, having to show identification. The guards allowed them to enter the room.

They walked up to Jan. She lay there resting with her eyes closed. Corene gently touched Jan's hand. Jan startled, jumped, and started to scream.

"Honey, it's us, Mom and Dad. Baby, we are here. Everything is okay."

"Oh, Mom, I am so happy to see both of you. I thought I'd never see you again."

"Don't talk now. Just rest. The man that did this to you is in jail. How are the others doing?"

"I think okay, except one. She hasn't woken up since we've been here."

"We want you to come home for awhile until you get back on your feet again."

"I am so confused about things. I don't know what to do now. This has messed up my mind and my life." Jan started to cry. "The only thing that kept me going was to dream about my future and my start into my new life. Now I don't know if I have a future."

"Honey, you will put this behind you very soon and be right back where you were."

Jan went to sleep. Corene could see the tears in the corner of her eyes.

Ken told Corene, "I will go to the cafeteria and get us a sandwich and some coffee. Let Jan sleep. She needs her rest."

When Ken returned, they ate and tried to be as quiet as they could.

The hours rolled by. Jan would jerk in her sleep every once in a while. Ken and Corene napped in the chairs provided in the room.

One of the nurses came in to do bed checks and vitals on the girls. They were restless and afraid of any sudden noise; their dreams were clearly troubled and would awaken them. The ordeal they had been through was so devastating that they just didn't know what mental scars it would leave. The nurse left in a hurry and soon returned to the room with what looked like one of the doctors. He checked one of the girls over and left the room. Two orderlies entered the room, and they transferred the girl to a gurney. All the tubes were removed, and machines were shut off.

Corene tried not to watch, but she opened her eyes slightly. She knew the girl had not survived, and she heard she was the first one buried and had received too much of the medicine that her body could not handle it. Now there would be a murder charge against Mr. Winters.

Corene had tears in her eyes, not knowing what meds had been administered to the girls. Corene began to pray for Jan and the other girls. She realized they needed to tell Jan, but they would wait until the next day. Maybe she would feel better.

The sunlight came in through the windows a few hours later. The three remaining girls woke up. They felt nauseated from the drugs. They were shaky and suffering from the side effects of the misused drugs. They noticed the bed was empty beside them and became upset, crying, screaming. The nurse and doctor came into the room. They calmed the girls down and explained what had happened. "Sandy was the first girl that had been buried. Her blood screen showed she had more of the paralyzing drug in her system. It kept her sedated and immobilized, and her body could not take the doses. It stopped her lungs and heart. You three need to start getting on your feet and walking around. The sooner you start normal activities and therapy, the sooner you can heal and put all this behind you."

Many family members came to see the other two girls, Beth and Ann. They helped with the girls walking and gave encouragement and advised that they follow their diets and drinking fluids. Within a week, all three girls were showing improvement.

Ken and Corene stayed with Jan, encouraging her during her recuperation period, all knowing the day to leave the hospital was soon approaching. After lunch, as they were laughing and visiting about past memories, three well-dressed men entered the room. They were detectives from the Burk law enforcement agency. They needed to ask some questions about what had happened. The girls were very reluctant to talk about it. Ann responded by crying. "It was just so terrifying. I thought I was dying and prayed I would."

Beth stated, "I was driving down the highway. I remember the tire going flat. I felt a sharp pain in my neck. When I awoke, my arm was burning, and it was dark, and I couldn't move. I don't know how long I lay there. It seemed like forever."

Jan entered the conversation. "I prayed for God to help me. When I felt the warmth of the sun, the light burned my eyes. I thought God had opened the door and come to get me."

After the girls told their stories, the detectives informed the girls, "The charges against Mr. Winters have been revised to murder in the first degree. He will never hurt anyone again. The district attorney is seeking the death penalty. We wish you the very best, and we will be in touch if you are needed to testify."

The detectives left, and they all started talking about their experiences. None of them knew where they were going from here. All they knew was they wanted to leave the hospital and go on with their lives.

The doctor came into the room. "Have the detectives been here to visit with you girls?"

"Yes, this afternoon," Beth answered.

"Well, in the morning, all three of you will be discharged. You can go home with no restrictions. However, I do suggest that all of you continue some kind of counseling, and by all means, continue going to church. God saved you girls for a reason. Good luck to all of you!"

CHAPTER 4

Corene awoke off and on during the night to check on her daughter. She was not sleeping very well. She was twitching and twisting and jerking. Corene noticed tears running down her face. She realized it would take a long time before Jan could return to her old self again. This would remain in all their minds for a very long time.

As light came early, the room lit up to smile on everyone, showing a brand-new day—the day each girl would start anew to regain their lives and make themselves whole again, to put this behind them and find happiness for their futures.

A knock on the door startled them, and the nurse came in carrying breakfast trays. "Good morning, ladies. Isn't it a beautiful day? The sun is shining, and I hear you get to go home today."

The girls smiled and thanked the nurse for breakfast.

"Girls, when you are ready, we have the showers next to your room ready. Just let me know."

Beth looked at Jan and Ann. "What will you do now? Are either of you afraid?"

Ann squirmed in her seat. "I'm going home with my parents. I don't know." Tears rolled down her face. "I'm afraid he will come back and find us."

Ken joined in the conversation to calm the girls. "Now all of you listen. I know this is a horrible thing, but this man will pay for his crime. You need to heal as quickly as you can and get on with your lives. Don't live in fear and give him the satisfaction of ruining your lives. He's not worth it. You girls deserve to move on and heal from this horrible ordeal."

Jan had tears filling her eyes that she couldn't see to eat her breakfast. "Come on, let's finish breakfast and take showers. We are going home today!"

The nurse returned with trays for Ken and Corene.

"Thank you so much. We needed some coffee. We have a long trip home. Everyone has been so nice to all of us through this ordeal."

"Well, I'm ready for a shower now," Beth blurted out in a very upbeat tone.

"Me too!" Jan smiled.

"Jan, go ahead. I'll gather up your belongings while you are taking your shower," Corene happily stated.

The girls prepared and headed for the showers. Beth's and Ann's families arrived to assist in getting them ready to go home.

"I am so glad that these girls have the family support. They are going to need this to get their lives back on track. It's going to take a long time and a lot of love." Ken had spoken up to the girls' families.

"Oh, I know. We have been to counselors ourselves for advice and suggestions. We are going to continue to provide as much help as we need to," Beth's father added.

"I just hope all the girls can regain everything that monster has taken from them." Ann's mother was in tears.

"Don't cry. We have to show victory, and the only way to show that is to provide strength for all the girls," Corene added.

The girls returned from the shower dressed and halfheartedly smiling. You could see fear and sadness beam from their faces. They stood looking at the empty bed where Sandy had lain. Sadness engulfed the room.

"It could have been one of us or all of us. I feel so sorry for her family and what they have to go through," Jan spoke up.

"Will we ever get past this?" Beth asked.

"Yes, we will work hard and win over this nightmare," Ann piped up.

The doctor walked in and handed the girls their records and discharge papers. "Now I highly recommend each of you get with a doctor in your towns and continue therapy. Continue to gain back your strength and get past this. I believe each of you have all the family support and positive encouragement. Good luck to all of you."

The girls hugged, and everyone started filing out of the room. As they neared the elevators, fear set in. How would they get out of the hospital? The elevator suddenly looked too small, too enclosed.

A nurse came up running behind them. "Girls, how about if one family at a time goes to the first floor?"

The girls thought a bit. "It's now or never. We can do this. What do you say?" Jan smiled.

The girls nodded. "Yeah, we've got this!"

Jan and her family walked toward the elevator. The nurse got on, and as she turned, she said, "You girls stay here, and I will return to assist you down."

As the elevator doors closed, Jan felt weak. "I can't breathe!"

"Don't panic. Breathe slowly in and out of your mouth."

The door came open, and Jan stepped out, gasping.

"See? Everything is fine, dear. Good luck, Jan."

The nurse returned to assist the families of Beth and Ann down to the first floor. Jan's dad went to bring the car to the front door. While Jan and her mother waited, the elevator bell rang. Beth and her family exited. Beth was crying, shaking, so frightened. "I can't do this! I can't make it!" Her mother, talking calmly, was trying to reassure her. "Honey, I am right here. Just take slow breaths." They walked over to where Jan and her mother were sitting.

The elevator bell rang again, and Ann exited with her family. She was clutching her mother, burying her head against her, shaking uncontrollably. The trauma the girls experienced was going to take a long time to get over and move on from, and they all became aware of this as they prepared to leave the hospital and go their own way.

"There is Dad with the car, dear. Let's get going."

Jan stood up, tears rolling down her cheeks. The three girls hugged, crying. "You two take care and get strong and well in a hurry. We can't let this ruin our lives!"

Jan turned to her mother. "Let's go, Mom. I am ready to go home."

Once in the car, Jan lay down on a soft pillow in the backseat, and her mom covered her with a soft blanket as they started down the highway toward home.

As Jan dozed off, she felt something sting her neck and saw Mark Winters's face. It was dark around her. She was cold and choking, her throat tight. Suddenly she jerked, screaming. Her dad pulled the car over to the side of the road. Her mother jumped into the backseat. "Calm down.

You just had a bad dream. I'm right here. I'm not going to leave you."

"Oh, Mom, it was just like I was living it all over again. I don't know if I will ever get over this!" Jan was crying hysterically, worried.

"You will, dear. I will stay back here on the ride home."

As her dad pulled back on the highway, thoughts ran through his mind. *Can we beat this? I can't imagine five days underground. How horrible.* He prayed, *God, help my daughter please.*

The ride home was quiet. Corene held her daughter, stroking her hair. As Jan rested quietly, she tried her best to stay awake so as not to remember. She felt better in her mother's arms. The trip seemed like it took forever.

"Jan, Corene, we are coming up to the house. Are you ready to go in?"

"Dad, is there anyone around? I don't want anyone to see me!"

"No, I don't see anyone."

As they pulled into the driveway, Jan felt a little anxious. She got out of the car and ran into the house and up the stairs to her room and closed the door.

Jan's parents unloaded the car and started to settle back into their home. Both were wondering, *Where will we go from here?*

"Honey, you know my friend Rick Petes? He is a psychologist. Maybe he can give us some ideas."

"Just don't rush her. Don't push."

"I'm not. I just want her to recover from this nightmare."

CHAPTER 5

As Jan lay curled up on the bed with Mr. Tuttles, tears were rolling down her face. *Why did this happen to me?* she thought. A light tap on the door startled Jan, and she started shaking and hugging Mr. Tuttles tighter than ever. A voice so loving and familiar to Jan eased her apprehension a bit.

"Jan, honey, it's Mom. I brought you something to eat." Corene spoke as softly and lovingly as she could.

As Corene entered the room, she noticed Jan was buried in the covers. All the lights were on, and she was squeezing Mr. Tuttles so hard that Corene thought the stuffed animal might burst open.

"Momma, what am I going to do?" She was crying hysterically. "I am so frightened. I'm not coming out of my room. I still see his face."

"Now, now, honey, everything's going to be fine. Your dad has this friend, and he may be able to help you get past this."

"No! I can't talk to anyone. I am too afraid! Help me, Momma. Tell me what to do!"

"You eat something and get some rest now. We can talk about all this later. I will talk to your father to see what he thinks." Corene left and returned to the dining room where Ken was eating, and joined him at the table.

"Ken, she doesn't want to come out of her room, and she definitely doesn't want to talk to anyone."

"Let me talk to Rick tomorrow when I get to work. Let her stay in her room, and don't push her. He may have some good advice. We need to get her back on her feet."

That evening was fairly quiet. At times they could hear Jan in her room crying and sobbing. They felt that maybe if she faced some of this on her own, she might get better faster. It was hard not to run to her side, but they knew she needed to build her strength and get her mind set on the future. Corene and Ken could not rest very well; they heard every noise Jan made.

The next morning Corene went to the kitchen to prepare breakfast. Ken got ready for work and went to the kitchen. Corene was making a tray for Jan.

"Good morning, sweetheart. Let me take Jan's breakfast to her. You sit down and enjoy your breakfast since you will be busy all day." Ken picked up the tray and headed up the stairs to Jan's room. He lightly tapped on the door. "Honey, it's Dad with your breakfast." He slowly opened the door to find Jan in a corner, squeezing the stuffing out of Mr. Tuttles. "Oh, honey, come and have some coffee and juice and eat some breakfast." He set the tray down and helped Jan to the bed, trying not to show the concern that was building in his heart.

"Daddy, I'm so scared!" Jan was crying hysterically.

"Honey, Mom will be here all day with you. I'm going to work, and you can call me if you want to. Now eat before your eggs get cold. I love you, baby!"

Ken went back to the dining room. "Oh, honey, this is going to be rough. You need to check on her often today. Here is her tray from last night."

"I know. It is so hard to see her this way, but I will sit with her. Maybe she can get some rest."

"Good breakfast, hon. I have to run. I'll call you later. I'll talk to Rick, and we will talk more tonight."

"Bye, honey!"

Ken was out the door and in the car.

Corene poured herself another cup of coffee and headed to Jan's room. She lightly tapped on the door. "It's Mom, honey." She turned the doorknob to enter the room. Jan was just finishing her breakfast.

"That was good, Mom, or I was pretty hungry."

"Well, you seem to be in a good mood. Are you feeling better?"

"I haven't been able to sleep much, so I have been doing a lot of thinking. I had a life until that man took it from me, so now I need to move on and take my life back. This is so hard, but I can do it."

"I know, dear, but we will get through this together." Drinking their coffee together, they reminisced and even laughed. Corene started to feel more at ease about the situation.

"Well, honey, you get some rest. I need to get some things done downstairs." Corene left smiling and happy that Jan was looking at the awful situation positively.

The day passed with Corene feeling good about things; however, Jan stayed in her room. Everything was going well. Corene fixed sandwiches, and they ate lunch in Jan's room together and visited. Corene did not want to push Jan, so they didn't talk about future plans.

"Mom, I know this is hard on us all, but I want to go on with my life. I do hope that someday I can forget that horrible incident."

"You will get past all this. You just have to take it one day at a time." After they ate, Corene started putting away the dishes. "I have some other things to do downstairs, and

I need to start dinner. Your dad will be home, hungry as a bear." Both laughed hysterically.

"Mom, I hope that someday I have a good home and man that really cares for me like Dad takes care of you."

"Yes, your dad is a good husband and father. I was really blessed. I don't know what I would do without him. Life has been very good for both of us."

Corene returned to her housework and started dinner about four. About six, Ken opened the front door and went into the house. "Honey, I'm home!" Laughing and walking into the kitchen to find his wife, he said, "Umh-umh! Something smells great. I'm sure it's one of your special creations."

"Oh you, you're such a romantic, and you always know the right things to say."

"No, I just have a special family. Speaking of, how was Jan today?"

"Great, we talked a couple of times today over coffee, lunch, and snacks. She was really in a good mood, wanting to move forward. I was so happy with her attitude today."

"I talked to Rick, and he said he would be glad to help. Matter of fact, if you don't mind, he will come to dinner tomorrow night and talk with Jan to see where we need to go from here. I told him she's not even coming out of her room, and he told me that was quite normal from these kinds of experiences."

"Sure, if it will help. We need to see what she needs to start her healing."

"When you fix her tray, I will take it up to her and tell her. I don't want any surprises to set her healing back."

"I will get her tray ready." Corene busied herself fixing Jan's dinner tray for Ken.

Ken picked up the tray and went to Jan's room, tapping lightly on her door and entering her room. "Hi, honey, here is your dinner tray. I need to talk to you about something."

"Okay, Daddy."

"I talked to Rick today, and he said he would be happy to help us. He is going to come for dinner tomorrow night and would very much like to talk to you to see what we can do to help you. What do you think?"

"Daddy, I don't know. It's all still so raw and fresh."

"He won't make you feel uncomfortable, and he won't pressure you. He just wants to have a short visit with you."

After some persuasion from her dad, Jan reluctantly agreed.

The next night, the doorbell rang. Corene went to the door. "Hello, Rick, it's good to see you again."

"Hi! Ken asked me to come and visit with Jan to see if I can be of some help."

"Oh, I pray you can help her through this."

"First, let's see if we can convince her to come to the table for dinner."

Corene led Rick to Jan's room. She knocked on the door and opened it slightly. "Honey, Rick is here to visit with us."

Jan started shaking as Rick entered the room. "Hi, Jan, it is so good to see you again."

"Hello, I am so sorry, but I just feel afraid all the time."

"Well, that's why I am here—to see if I can help you get your life back. First thing, Jan, let's all go downstairs to the dining room and have dinner together so I can get a feel of where you are now."

"No! I can't! Don't you make me! I have to stay here!"

"Jan, I know this was a horrible experience for you, but do you want to spend your valuable life a prisoner to this man and stay here just reliving that horrible event?"

"No! I am weak. Not strong enough to fight this."

"Honey, we are here with you. We will all help you get past this."

Jan looked at them for the longest time; then she swung her legs off the bed and started to stand up. Weak at the thought of going downstairs, her knees buckled. Ken caught her and helped her stand back up.

"Easy now. Just hang onto me, and we will walk down to the table together."

As they left the room and slowly headed down the stairs to the dining room, Jan stopped, looking around as though it was the first time seeing anything around her.

Rick said gently, "Now, Jan, I can talk and help you as much as I can, but you need to be positive about your progress and start to develop who you are and what your dreams are for your future. You need to do the work to get yourself back on track. You can do this. We will work hard together."

Corene gave the evening meal prayer and thanked God for blessing them with Rick to help Jan.

Rick began to visit with Ken about his job and the day he had. Then he looked at Jan, who was beginning to eat. "Jan, what do you think about what your dad just shared about his job?"

"My father is very successful, and I know he likes his job at the paper. It has sufficiently supported our family for several years."

"Very good. I believe that you will be a very successful designer as well."

"Oh, I don't know if I can continue now."

"The next step is to be positive and strive towards what you want to do!"

Dinner went well. Jan continued to express her opinions and join in their conversation. Rick visited with the family to get a vision of the family as a whole.

When dessert was over, Rick drank his coffee and commented, "I have enjoyed this excellent dinner. Thank you for inviting me. Jan, I have an assignment for you for tomorrow. I want you to come out of your room for all three of your meals and then assist your mother in cleaning up after each meal for the next couple of days, then add helping your mother prepare dinner. I will return in a couple of nights for dinner, and we will discuss how this worked for you."

"Isn't this too much all at once?" Ken asked, looking at Rick.

"I see a solid family relationship. Now I need to see how much she can do on her own. It will show her that she does have the strength to move on and not go into a depression from her fear."

"I will try my best!" Jan added.

Rick got up and excused himself, walking toward the door. "See all of you in two nights."

Jan got up from the table and headed toward her room slowly, questioning her ability to go on.

Morning came. Jan got up, saying to herself, *I've got to do this. I've got to do this.* She made her bed and straightened her room. Opening her door and walking toward the kitchen, she saw her mother and father.

"Good morning, Mom and Dad. I made it!"

"We are so proud of you!"

Jan walked to the stove and got her breakfast and went to the table to eat, still saying to herself, *I can do this.*

"Well, girls, have a great day. I'm off. See you tonight after work!"

Jan finished her breakfast and went to the sink to clean up the dishes. As she washed the dishes, her mind wandered off to what she wanted to do with her life, not realizing she was smiling.

"Mom, I think I will bake some cookies. I feel like today is a cookie day!"

"Are you sure you are ready?"

"I am ready to move on. Rick's right. I need to be positive."

Jan jumped in and made some chocolate chip cookies, which were her favorite. Then she started making a sandwich lunch for her and her mom. When Corene returned and saw what Jan had done, she was so shocked.

"What's this?"

"This, Mom, is lunch today! Sandwiches, salad, tea, and my favorite—homemade chocolate chip cookies!" Jan was laughing.

"I am so excited, dear. You are so positive today!"

As they ate, they giggled and talked about the future. It had been so long since they laughed together. After lunch, Jan cleaned the kitchen and put all the dishes away. She walked into the laundry room, where Corene was folding and ironing.

"Let me help you, Mom. I have to keep pushing myself to move on."

"I just don't want you to do too much too fast!"

The day zipped right by. Jan had stayed out of her room all day. She followed her mother to the kitchen when it was time to start dinner. Jan jumped right in to assist her mother in preparing dinner. They talked and laughed as they worked. They were having a great time.

At six thirty sharp, the front door opened, and Ken came in. Jan ran to greet her father at the door.

"Hello, missy, what have you been up to?"

"Dad, I baked cookies, I made lunch, and I cleaned up the kitchen. I even helped Mom with laundry, and then I helped cook dinner! I have not been in my room all day!"

"Oh, Jan! I am so proud of you. I knew you could do it," Ken said, hugging his daughter with pride. He followed his daughter to the dining room, where dinner was waiting.

Corene entered the dining room. "Hi, honey. How was your day?"

"Great, sweetheart. I hear that Jan and you had quite an eventful day."

"Oh yes, it was a great day."

They all sat down to the table and gave grace, thanking God for his help in this situation. They laughed and talked through dinner with a newfound happiness. Ken knew the worst was behind them. After dinner, Jan cleaned up the kitchen, then entered the living room afterward. Ken and Corene were watching television.

Jan stated, "I am kind of tired. I think I will go to bed. Good night."

"Good night, sweetheart. Glad you had a good day!"

In unison, Ken and Corene looked at each other.

"Honey, is Jan going to be okay? I'm worried."

"Corene, I think she wants to move on. She just needed permission and to really know that it was okay to move on."

The next morning Jan jumped up out of bed again and headed for the kitchen for breakfast. "Good morning. Boy, did I sleep well!"

Corene smiled at her daughter from across the dinner table. "That is great. What's on your mind for today?"

"Well, while you girls decide the work list for today, I had better get myself to work. Love you both. Have a great day!"

Jan jumped up to hug her father and returned to her breakfast. When she had finished eating, she cleaned the kitchen and went to find her mother. Corene was vacuuming the living room. Jan motioned to her mom, and Corene shut the vacuum off.

"Mom, I am going to clean the upstairs."

"Okay, that would be a big help."

Jan busied herself cleaning the upstairs. She joined her mother in the kitchen later for lunch, and after lunch, she cleaned the kitchen.

"Rick will be joining us for dinner again tonight. I wonder what his next assignment will be."

"You never know, but he is very concerned about your progress, I do know that."

Jan began planning and getting together the things that she needed for dinner. The day zipped by, and again for the second day, Jan had been successful in staying out of her room. She prepared dinner and set the table, making sure to include an extra setting for Rick.

At six thirty, the door opened, and two people entered, not just Ken this time. Rick was with him.

"I have been bursting with excitement, unable to contain or wait to see how you have been doing."

"I think you will be very shocked tonight. Let's go to the table for dinner first."

Once in the dining room, she burst out, "I did it all by myself!"

"You did? That's great! Tell me about these past two days."

They sat down to give grace for the meal, thanking God for the progress. Jan began to tell Rick all about the two days. She was upbeat and so excited to be telling about the things she had done.

"That is so great, and I feel a great boost of excitement and energy from you since I first saw you."

"I want to thank you, Rick. It just amazes me the changes in Jan in such a short amount of time. She has perked up and is doing so much better."

He smiled, then turned back to Jan. "Dinner is very good, Jan. Thank you for all your strong efforts and for having me for dinner. Now I have a new assignment for you. On Sunday morning, I would like for you to attend church with your parents. Then Monday morning, go grocery shopping with your mother."

"Oh, Rick, being here inside is one thing. I'm not sure I am ready to go outside yet."

"You have conquered not staying in your room all day. There is nothing left to challenge you in the house. It is time to go outside. You must go out in order to conquer the outside world. I will be back next week to see how it goes."

"I know what you are doing, and I'm also not sure that anything will ever erase the memory of what happened."

"You can't erase the memories. You have to accept them and learn to live with them without the fears."

"Okay, I will try. Besides, I won't be alone. Mom and Dad will be with me."

"That's right. You must realize you are never alone!"

CHAPTER 6

Sunday morning arrived, and Jan and her parents ate breakfast, laughed, and discussed the plans for the day.

"You know, I feel real good about my progress, and I know that it will turn out all right."

"How about after church, we go to your favorite restaurant for lunch?" Jan's dad asked.

"That sounds like it might be a good idea. I am anxious to get on with my life and hope for the best that everything will start falling back into place!"

"I am so proud of you, dear. I know it will all get back to the way it used to be. However, we had better get ready for church. We don't want to be late," her mother added.

As they prepared for church, Ken went out to get the car and pull up to the front of the house. Out the door Jan and her mother bounded, and they were off to church.

Once inside the church, many friends and acquaintances greeted Jan and her parents. Everyone was so polite and courteous by not bringing up Jan's ordeal; everyone was pleased to see them. When church ended, they drove to the restaurant and had a wonderful lunch. The day went by so joyfully and uneventfully; the family had peace that Jan was recovering very well. The next day, Jan was up and preparing for the day's activity—shopping with her mother. They went to the mall, where Jan bought a few things and ran into a few of her friends. She invited them to come by the house to visit later.

"Maybe it is time you go out and spend time with your friends," her mother suggested.

"I agree. However, I am nervous, but it is time to lay it down and go on with my life."

The next couple of weeks, Jan was out by herself or with her friends shopping, taking in movies, eating out; it was almost like nothing had happened. No one ever mentioned it, and Jan was as vibrant as she had always been.

Several weeks passed. The mail came, and there was an envelope for Jan from Jordan. It was from Bentley Design Today. Corene froze in her tracks. "Jan, come here please!"

"What's wrong, Momma?"

Tears were rolling down Corene's face. "What is this, Jan?"

"Momma, I was going to tell you, but I decided to wait and see if I got the job first."

Jan tore open the envelope and read the letter. Her eyes lit up like a candle. "Mom, I got the job!"

"Are you sure this is what you want? Are you sure you are ready to move so far away?"

"Yes, Momma! I have to, or I'll never know if I can do it on my own. I'll never know if I don't just get out there and do it."

"Does your father know yet?"

"No, I will show him the letter tonight."

As six thirty came, Jan was very nervous about talking to her father, but she knew she had to.

Ken came home from work excited to see his family and have a peaceful evening like every other night.

"Hi, Daddy! I have something to talk to you about."

"Okay, honey, what is it?"

Jan handed the envelope to her dad. His eyes widened in shock as he opened it and read the letter. "You took a job in Jordan? That's farther away than before. Do you know what you are doing?"

"Yes, Daddy, this is what I need to do. You can't take care of me all my life. I have to get out on my own and make it."

"Let's go eat and discuss this more. I'm just not sure you're ready for all this."

They ate dinner while making small talk, chatting about things like how their days had gone. Jan was even more nervous about after dinner, when she had to discuss her move and taking a job so far away. When dinner was over, Ken looked at Jan.

"Help your mother clean up and come into the living room, where we can discuss this matter further."

He got up from the table and entered the living room. Jan and Corene went to the kitchen to clean up, and when they finished, they joined Ken in the living room. He looked so perplexed and uncertain, but as he saw them, he smiled. "I've given this matter a lot of thought, and yes, you are right to continue your life."

"I knew you would understand, Daddy."

Corene started to cry, worried about her daughter.

"Corene, what I thought is, we will get her packed and move her to Jordan ourselves. I can get a week off work. That way, we can find her a nice place and get her started off on the right foot."

"Oh, that's an excellent idea, Ken. Are you sure you can get time off from the paper?"

"I know they will understand. This time, we will do things the right way."

Jan jumped up and hugged her dad's neck. "I knew you would understand!"

The next day, Ken went to work and put in his request for the next week off. Corene and Jan went shopping for things that Jan would need. Jan visited her friends to let them know she would be moving soon. The rest of the week was very busy for Jan as she started packing to prepare for her move.

"Mr. Tuttles, we are moving, and this time, it's going to be great. Dad and Mom are coming with us." She hugged Mr. Tuttles and jumped on the bed.

The day came. The trailer was backed into the driveway. Ken, Corene, and Jan started loading all the boxes, suitcases, and furniture out of Jan's room until it was completely empty.

"Okay, let's hit the road to Jordan!" Ken stated.

"Corene, you ride with Jan in her car, and I'll drive our car and pull the trailer."

So they pulled out of the drive, following each other like a caravan, and Mr. Tuttles was in the backseat. The trip was long and tiring, but they steadily continued. By lunchtime, they had arrived at a roadside restaurant, where they stopped for lunch.

"How are you girls doing?" Ken asked.

"Oh, we are laughing and visiting, having a great time, Daddy."

"I sure will miss these times, sweetheart!" Corene's voice cracked as she choked back the tears.

"Oh, Mom, now you need to develop time for yourself. No more raising kids and just being a housewife. Enjoy your freedom!"

"Wait a minute, honey. She still has a husband to take care of!" her dad interjected.

Laughing, they entered the restaurant. It was turning into a very enjoyable trip, and the weather was beautiful.

After lunch, they hit the road again. The afternoon hours were long, but Corene and Jan didn't mind. As the miles were behind them, the hours clicked by. It was starting to get dark. A town was in their vision. Ken pulled the car into a motel parking lot that had an adjoining restaurant, and Jan pulled in behind him and parked. Ken went inside and got a room for them for the night. It was dinnertime, so they decided to check out the restaurant next door.

"We'll stay here tonight and get a good night's rest and go on into Jordan tomorrow," Ken informed his wife and daughter.

As they enjoyed their dinner, they laughed and visited. "I have a surprise for you, Jan," Ken informed his daughter. "I know a real estate agent in Jordan. I met him a few years ago while I did an article in that area. Anyway, I gave him a call, and he found you a house in Jordan."

"Really, Dad? I don't have to live in an apartment?"

"No, and I got a real good deal on it. I think you will love it, and your mother can help you decorate it this week."

"Oh, Daddy, I love you! How can I ever repay you?"

"Just be happy and enjoy your job and get back to living a full life."

Ken got up and paid the bill, and they went to their motel room.

"Let's get some rest so we can get into Jordan in the morning."

Jan was all excited to see the house her dad had found for her. She went right to sleep thinking about the new life awaiting her in Jordan.

Morning came quickly. Jan was busily showering and dressing to go eat breakfast. Corene was almost ready when Jan came out of the bathroom. "Come on, Mom. Let's go eat while Dad is getting ready. He can join us when he's dressed."

"Sounds like someone is excited."

"Oh, I am!"

Corene and Jan walked to the restaurant and sat down to order. By the time they received their food and started eating, Ken had arrived. "Hurry, guys, so we can get started." Jan was giddy.

"We have to get gas and check out, then we will be on our way."

About an hour later, they were on the road toward Jordan. They still had a few hours driving time. The closer they got, the more excited Jan was. She was excited to see the house; she knew her dad had done a very wonderful thing, and the house would be big enough for them to come and visit, and with what happened to Jan, that would probably be often.

Ken called ahead to his friend Jim. "Hi, Jim, this is Ken, and we are about an hour outside of Jordan. Can you meet us at the house in about an hour and a half? I'd like to unload this trailer and start getting Jan settled today."

"Sure, Ken, it was great doing business with you, and we have it cleaned and ready for her to move right in."

"Great, I can't thank you enough. See you in a little while."

"Bye."

As they pulled into the city limits of Jordan, Ken turned toward Jan's new house. When they pulled up to the house, there was Jim sitting in the driveway waiting for them.

Jan and Corene got out of the car. Jan's eyes were wide with excitement.

"Oh, how beautiful!" she screeched.

There in front of Jan stood a beautiful three-bedroom house. The front yard was manicured and green, with rosebushes and beautiful flowers in the flower beds. One tree stood proudly by the drive, shaped and trimmed up nicely.

Jim handed the keys to the front door to Jan. "Are you ready to go and see the inside?"

"Oh yes, it is breathtaking. I can't believe what I am seeing."

"Also, Jan, you are only a few blocks away from your job, so you could choose to walk and save gas," Jim replied. They all laughed.

Going inside, Jan was shocked. There were new carpets, and the house was spotless. The kitchen had a built-in stove, oven, and microwave. The refrigerator was in place. All Jan needed was her dishes and food, and she was set to prepare a meal.

"Mom, did you know Dad did all this?"

"Honey, we talked about it and decided it was a good idea for you to have your own place, but I left it all up to him."

Jim told all, "Congratulations, kids. I've got to run, but if you have any problems or need anything, just let me know."

"Thanks again, Jim, for everything," Ken stated.

CHAPTER 7

Ken started unloading the trailer while Corene and Jan looked around the house and the backyard.

"This is just gorgeous, Mom! I love you both!"

"Honey, we just want you to be happy and have a good start."

As they entered the house, they heard the doorbell ring. There in the entryway stood a man dressed in work clothes. They walked up to him.

Her dad made the introductions. "Honey, Jan, this is David Kent. Jim helped me find him. He is going to keep up the landscaping and keep an eye out so that there aren't any problems. Also, if anything breaks, he will get it repaired."

"Wow, Dad, This is entirely too much!"

"Honey, you have your job to think about, and I want to know things will be take care of around here."

"No problems, Mr. Williams. I will be happy to keep up with things," David said with a friendly smile.

Ken took David around to look at the house and the backyard. "If you see any problems or anyone hanging around that shouldn't be, call me and the police at once!"

"I promise. I will check in on her and let you know that everything is okay!"

Ken took out his checkbook and wrote him a check for the first month. "Jan can pay you the next month."

"Thank you. I will do a good job for you!" David left to work at one of the other houses in the neighborhood.

Ken went back into the house. "Let's get these things put away, and by the time we get that done, it will be time to take the trailer back to the lot, find a bite of supper, and come back and relax for today. I'm sure we are all worn out."

"Yeah, can you believe all this? It's crazy," Jan said.

They all jumped in, and in no time at all, they had everything unloaded and placed where it should be.

"When we get back, we can make a list of what you need and go shopping tomorrow," Corene said.

They all jumped in the car and drove to the trailer company where they rented the trailer, got the trailer unhooked, and turned it in. When they drove to a nearby restaurant, they were all laughing and giggling, exhausted from the day's events.

When they pulled into the driveway, it was already getting dark. It was time to bring the day's events to a close. They all flopped down to the makeshift furniture placed around.

"Tomorrow we will go shopping and get more furniture in this house."

"How long are you and Mom staying before you go back home? I need to check in with my job in a few days. I start work on Monday."

"We will head back home after we get the house ready and you settled in and make sure your job is going okay."

They talked for a few more minutes, then her mom said, "Let's get to bed and get some sleep."

The morning sun smiled brightly through the windows, waking the family, and each one was smiling and happy for one more day together.

"Okay, ladies, are we ready to get some breakfast and start some shopping? Say, how about we get some food in this house and eat our meals here?"

"Great, Dad, maybe things will slow down so we can enjoy the town." All laughing about how consumed they had been with things, they drove off to a breakfast house to eat.

"Jan, do you have any preference when it comes to furniture?"

"Well, Mom, I have never thought about it much, but we can look around to see what our choices are."

After breakfast, they drove down into the shops and soon came to a furniture store. They found a convenient parking place and went into the store.

"Oh my, what beautiful furniture. Dad, it's probably very expensive. Do you want to find a cheaper store?"

"Do you see furniture here that you need?"

"Yes, and I love all of it!"

"That's my girl. Let's get to shopping!"

Jan found a living room suite, a dining room suite, a master bedroom set, an office set, a TV room set, and one more guest room set. Each set was absolutely beautiful and ready for the store to pack and move.

A saleswoman approached them. "Young lady, we have appliances on the second floor if you are in need of a washer and dryer!"

"Dad, what do you think?"

"Absolutely! You have to do laundry. We need a stove and refrigerator so you can feed your hungry 'ole dad and mom!"

Laughing, they grabbed each other by the hand, and up the escalator they went. They soon found all the appliances they needed, as well as small appliances, and requested for everything to be delivered to Jan's new home.

"How long will it be before these things will arrive? So we can make sure we are there," Ken said.

"The store coordinator will start having the delivery people pack up and fill a truck one at a time, and when one truck returns, a second will go out until they have delivered all your purchases. My guess? The first truck should arrive in an hour."

"Well, we had better get to the house and get ready for delivery."

Soon after arriving home, the phone company arrived and installed the phones and set up the computer system. Then the cable company installed the cable on all the televisions that Jan planned for.

"It's almost lunch. How about a pizza, Dad, since we haven't gone grocery shopping yet?"

"Call and order the pizza. Don't forget the soda, girl!"

They busily moved about the furniture that they had brought in to make room for the deliveries. The doorbell rang. The pizza had arrived, and right behind the pizza, the first delivery truck backed into the driveway.

"We will try to get everything delivered today, but if not, it may take until tomorrow. We can deliver up to six this evening, and we will let you know when we have made the last load today."

Ken nodded. "That is great, guys. We would like the beds and appliances for sure, if we could at least get them today."

"I think we have some of the small appliances in each load."

Very shortly, the four men had unloaded the truck and were setting up the complete sets of furniture by room; they set up and installed everything brought in. The first truck pulled out, and the second truck backed in. Four men were also present, unloading and installing and setting up everything. With each load, the house looked more and more like a home.

The second truck pulled out, and the third truck backed in. Four men unloaded and installed and set up. As the Williamses' directed the movers and set everything in its place, they enjoyed their pizza.

"Mr. Williams, the boss said one more truck today. Tomorrow, they will bring the rest."

"That will be fine."

They watched the fourth truck back in, and within an hour, they were setting up. The day had gone by at maximum speed, much to all their surprise. The appliances were working and in place, the beds set up, the TVs working, and Jan's office set up. It was looking more like home. As the last truck drove away, they sat down on what living room furniture had been delivered.

"Girls, I am about worn out. We still need groceries. You're going to need some pictures, decorations, and more linen. We need to get going! Time's a-wastin'!" All laughing, they headed for the shopping center. They were in one store and out until they had the car so full, it looked like it was going to burst. They headed back home. Each one felt like a pack horse, carrying all the bags into the house.

"You girls start supper. I am going to hang pictures and hang drapes, and you can tell me if I'm wrong or where you want things."

Ken proceeded to put blinds on the windows. He had ideas on where some of the things went, so those items he could handle. Corene and Jan unpacked the groceries and put them away and began preparing their evening meal. When the dining room table was set and everything was ready, Corene went to find Ken to look at his progress. Jan was looking around at what her dad had been doing. The family hugged each other. "What do you think, baby?"

"It all looks great, Dad, but so much work!"

"It will all be done before I leave, sweetie."

They all entered the dining room for dinner. As they bowed their heads in prayer, Jan ended by saying, "Thank you, God, for such great parents. I am so blessed." As they ate their dinner, they discussed the next day's plans and what was left to do to get their little girl settled in her new life.

Corene smiled at Jan. "It is a privilege to do this for you. We want everything to go smoothly for you, dear."

They were all tired, so they decided to watch some television and shower and go to bed. They had yet another full and busy day ahead of them.

As the sun peaked through the blinds and lit up the beautiful rooms, they arose to head for the kitchen, where Jan made coffee with her new coffeemaker and started frying eggs and preparing the family's breakfast. They enjoyed the beginning of the day. Though they were still tired from the trip and the shopping and fixing the house, they were eager to complete the chores ahead of them.

Jan's dad stood up. "We had better get things cleaned up. The trucks will start arriving here very soon." Scrambling to their feet, everyone started in cleaning and rearranging and making up beds and getting ready for the rest of the furniture to arrive.

As each truck arrived, everyone was patient and steadily worked until the very last piece was unloaded. They all took deep breaths, including the workers. *That was quite the job*, they all thought, looking at each other. Finally, it was a home with everything in place, and maybe just one more day of shopping would conclude everything. Ken could finish the trimming and let Corene and Jan do their shopping.

"I will fix us some lunch." Jan skipped off to the kitchen. Corene followed to help and to set the table. Ken came in and sat down at the table, and they began to eat lunch. "Now isn't this better than having to run out to get something to eat?"

"I think so!" Corene and Jan agreed.

After lunch, they cleaned up and decided to go to the bank to open an account for Jan. "You girls go do that and finish your shopping. I am going to finish hanging drapes and decorating. I will see you when you get back." Ken handed Jan a check. "Here, honey, is some money to keep you going until you get your first check."

"Dad, you have to stop this. You will be broke!"

"Nah, we are okay. Besides, you are my only daughter, and I want to help you get started."

Off in the bank where Jan opened her bank account, everyone was very friendly and welcomed Jan to Jordan. "This seems like a very friendly town. I think I'm going to like it here."

"If there is ever anything we can do for you, please let us know!"

Leaving the bank, Corene and Jan headed for the mall. Once inside, Jan turned in circles. "Oh, Mom, I think I am dreaming. This is absolutely beautiful. Everything is so beautiful."

"I know, dear, this is terrific. Now let's do what we women do best—shopping!"

"Yeah, let's do some shopping!"

Jan was first one in the mall, trying on clothes and shoes and looking at everything they could in every store.

It was not long until they both were weighed down by their purchases.

"What do we do, Mom? Put everything in the car and come back in?"

A mall guard overheard their conversation. "No, ma'am, we have carts right over there to put your packages in, and you can keep shopping and use the cart to take to your car."

"Wow, Mom, I don't know if that's a good idea. A person could go broke!" They were both laughing as the guard brought them a cart.

"Have a great day, ladies!"

Corene and Jan spent most of the day right there, putting their packages in the cart and going in and out of one store after another. "Jan, it is dark. Your father will think we are lost. Do you think you have everything you need to start your new job? I don't know of anything that we have overlooked."

"I am tired as well. Let's head home. Dad is probably starving. I know I'm hungry."

They pushed the cart to the car, loading all their purchases inside. Again the backseat and trunk were full. After returning the cart, they headed home. Ken, patiently waiting, came out to help unload the bags.

The girls started supper, and before long, they sat down to a good home-cooked dinner. Each one was hungry and exhausted from the day's events.

"Tomorrow, I need to go by the job and check in. Do you and Mom want to go with me?"

"We would love to, but don't you think your first impression should not be with your mom and dad?"

"Well, I guess you are right. I should go alone. Mom, will you help me hang up clothes and put the things away after we clean the kitchen?"

"Sure I will, sweetie."

"This is a great dinner, girls. I have enjoyed this week. It's been a lot of fun. I think tomorrow I can finish everything. While you check out your job, Mom and I can finish up things."

After dinner, Corene and Jan cleaned up the kitchen, then carried the bags up the stairs. Ken jumped up and grabbed some of them as well and carried them up the stairs. "You girls have fun now. I'm going to watch some television and rest."

They started going through the purchases, laughing and giggling, putting up things as they came to it.

"Mom, I'm excited about tomorrow, and I am scared all at the same time."

"You'll do great, dear. Don't worry about a thing."

CHAPTER 8

Morning came quickly. Everyone was awake and up for breakfast with the sun. Jan was very nervous about going to her job.

"Jan, go ahead and shower and get ready. I will clean up the kitchen."

"Thank you, Mom! You're a peach! Oh, I am so nervous about this. It's what I have always wanted, and now it's here." Jan ran off to her room to get ready.

Corene stayed behind sipping her coffee. "My, how our little girl has grown. Time is just passing us by."

Ken looked up from his eggs and toast. "Now don't get all mushy on me. It's no different than her first day of school."

"I know, and that was only yesterday."

Corene busied herself cleaning the kitchen while Ken started in with hanging more curtains and doing the finishing touches about the house. It was really looking nice, and Ken knew it would spark up Jan's life with a new start. Ken noticed that David had arrived and started mowing and trimming in the yard. It surprised Ken to see him there that early.

Jan came bouncing down the stairs all ready. Corene met her at the bottom of the stairs. "Knock 'em dead, honey. They will just love you, and everything will be okay."

"I'm off, and I'll get back here to help with the house as soon as I can." Out the door she went and in her car to drive to Bentley Designs for Today. Excitement and anxiousness thrilled her; she could feel her heart pulsing inside her chest as she parked in the Bentley parking lot. As she went through the door, she spotted the restrooms and decided one more look was in order. Coming out after one last look at herself, she got on the elevator to the third floor. The excitement of now having her own job still took priority over the fears she once had with the elevator. As the doors opened, she saw the receptionist and approached the desk.

"Hi, I'm Jan Williams. I was recently hired by Mr. Bentley, and now I'm here to visit with him about the job."

"Oh, yes, Jan, he told me this morning you would be coming in. Have a seat, and I will tell him you have arrived."

A few minutes later, a tall, slender, well-dressed man approached her. "Good morning, Jan. It is so good to see you. I'm Mike Bentley, owner and manager of Bentley

Designs for Today. Won't you come into my office, and we can talk?"

"It is so good to meet you, and I am so excited about this opportunity to start a design job."

They went into Mike's office, where they got acquainted and visited casually. "Well, let's get your paperwork done and show you your new office."

A younger man entered the office. "This is Ben Young. He is our relations manager, and he will take you over and finish your paperwork and give you a tour, then we'll see you Monday bright and early."

Jan shook Mike's hand and followed Ben to his office. He handed Jan a bunch of papers to fill out, took a snapshot for her badge to check in and out with, and then proceeded to give her the tour and show her what would now be her new office.

"This is so fabulous! A dream come true!" Jan was on cloud nine, floating in the air. Ben was laughing at her. "We are so glad to have such enthusiasm here. You sound like a real neat person to be around."

A head poked in the door. It was a pretty young girl from a few offices down. "Hi! I'm Chrissie. I will be on hand to assist you with any problems you may run into."

"Absolutely! Great to meet you. I'm sure I will need both of your help!"

Chrissie smiled at her, then turned to Ben. "Are we having coffee later, Ben?"

"When we get to that part of the morning, we will all meet in the cafeteria, so I will see you later."

"Okay, see you two later." Chrissie left and went down the hallway.

"Is that your girlfriend? She seems like a very sweet girl."

"No, we are just good friends. We hang out sometimes, but we don't date. We are married to the job."

"Oh, I see. Nothing wrong with that. I think I am going to enjoy being part of this. It seems like a great place to work!"

As they continued to work through the morning finishing Jan's employment file, she was so excited and felt she had already made two good friends. About eleven, they went to the cafeteria. There sat Chrissie having coffee and a muffin.

"Hey guys, the muffins are great today. You should try them."

Ben and Jan got their coffee and muffins and sat down with Chrissie. "Well, Jan, what do you think about the place?"

"Oh, I am so excited, and I love it here. I think I have met two good friends."

"Ben, who did you introduce her to?"

All three started laughing.

"You goof! She means you and me!"

They were all still laughing.

"You two are going to have to come over and hang out at my house sometime. Yes, my parents are here with me now, getting it all set up for me."

"Wow! We have apartments, and that's like living in someone's closets. The walls are paper-thin."

The three new friends sat laughing and visiting to get acquainted. Jan felt very comfortable and was very happy, hoping that everything stayed this way.

"Jan, I think all of your paperwork is ready now. If anything comes up, I will let you know, and we can take care of it."

"So I can go now? I need to get back and help my parents with the house. You two can come over and meet my parents and see my house after work. Matter of fact, come over for dinner."

"Sounds like a great plan. We will be there about six."

"Great, see you then."

Jan went out to the parking lot, got into her car, and drove home. As she walked in the house, her eyes got as big as saucers. "Mom, it's great. You two have been working all day on this?"

"Yes, dear, your father is a slave driver." Laughing, she asked, "How was your morning, dear?"

"Oh, it was great! I met two new friends that work with me. It's going to be really great. Matter of fact, I invited them over to meet you and Dad and have dinner with us tonight."

"Well, we better get in the kitchen and decide what we are going to have for dinner."

Ken appeared from upstairs. "What's all the excitement about down here?"

"We are having company for dinner tonight. Jan met two new friends, and they are coming to meet us."

"Hey, that's great! That's my girl, getting right into the game!"

They entered the kitchen to start dinner and set the table for their company. They decided on sandwiches for lunch and ate at the bar in the kitchen.

"The house looks great, Dad!"

"We kept on it all morning, and I think you will enjoy living here and be comfortable."

As six o'clock got closer, they had everything ready for dinner. Jan had changed into something more comfortable from work clothes. She had looked around the house and outdoors. Everything was great. The doorbell rang. Jan ran down the stairs to answer the door. Ken and Corene followed her to the doorway.

"Hi, guys, I am glad you made it!"

"Hey, Jan, this place is great. Right out of a magazine! It's beautiful."

"Thanks to my parents. Ben and Chrissie, this is my dad Ken Williams and my mom, Corene Williams. They have been here all week working on everything to get me set up here."

Corene extended her hand. "We are so glad to meet you, and we are so happy to know that Jan has already made two friends. Come in. Jan, show your friends the house, and then we will sit down to dinner."

As they went through the rooms, laughing and having a great time, they were so happy to have met Jan as well. They entered the dining room, all gathering around the table. Ken led them in prayer.

As they were enjoying fellowship together, visiting and getting to know one another, Ken said, "I want you two to know I expect you to look out for our little girl."

Ben nodded. "You bet, Mr. Williams. Jan is great, and we look forward to working with her and getting to know her better."

The evening drew to a close; it was getting late, so Ben and Chrissie decided it was time to leave. "We had a great evening. Dinner was great, and your parents are super people. We will see you at work Monday morning. Bye!" Out the door they bounced and into their cars.

"Dad, what do you think of Ben and Chrissie?"

"They are nice, and I hope the three of you can become close friends."

"I better help Mom clean up."

The rest of the evening was quiet. Jan was so happy about everything. She couldn't make it any better, even though she knew she would miss her parents when they went back home. The remaining days through the week's end, they drove, sightseeing and enjoying the town. They went bowling and enjoyed being together. They went shopping at the mall and the grocery store. Each day they were tired and rested when getting back to the house. Ken took pictures of the events and around the house. He got a beautiful photo album after developing the pictures. It made a great housewarming gift for Jan.

On Sunday, they all dressed up and went to the Christian Church, where Jan would be continuing her spiritual life. Ken took his family to a restaurant for Sunday dinner. Jan was so proud and happy; everything was fitting into place. Her life felt complete, even with her knowing her parents would soon be leaving.

Monday morning came fast. They all met at the breakfast table. Corene had prepared coffee and breakfast. She looked sad. "Jan, we will be going home this morning after we straighten up for you and clean up after breakfast."

"I know. It is for the best. I have to move on, and everything feels right."

"We will miss you, dear," Ken added.

They visited through breakfast and drank another cup of coffee. "Well, I need to get dressed for work." Jan went upstairs and took a quick shower and began getting ready for work.

Ken and Corene went about straightening, cleaning up after breakfast. Jan came down and met them in the front entryway, where they expressed their sad good-byes. "You have a good first day at work. Call us if you need anything, and we will be back to visit."

"Good-bye, Mom and Dad! Have a safe trip home. I will miss you. Love you! And thank you for everything."

"We love you!"

Jan went to her car and drove to work. Ken and Corene finished cleaning up and packed. Ken loaded the car and took one more look around. They got in the car and headed to the city limits to head for home.

CHAPTER 9

Jan looked forward to going to work every day. She was getting closer and closer to her new friends Ben and Chrissie. In the evenings, they went to each other's houses for dinner and games. On Sundays, they attended church together and spent a lot of time together. The three became so close that they were inseparable. They did everything together. Jan was so happy. Her life was going in the right direction. She couldn't ask for it to be any better, and her fears were gone.

Jan had been with the company for six months, and she had developed a very good reputation in her department of design. As she sat at her desk finishing a design, her phone rang.

"Good morning, Mr. Bentley. Why yes, I can come to your office. Give me a few minutes. I'm right in the middle of a project."

As Jan hung up the phone, she wondered what was going on as she had never been called to Mr. Bentley's office before. She left her office and walked to the elevator and pressed the button for the third floor. Still a little anxious about what was going on. She got off the elevator on the third floor and walked down the hall to Mr. Bentley's office. The receptionist smiled as she knew Jan. "I have heard some pretty good things about you."

"Thank you, I am glad."

"I'll let Mr. Bentley know you are here." As she put the phone down, she said, "You may go right in."

Jan entered the office. She saw two men and started to become nervous.

Mr. Bentley gestured for her to sit down. "Jan, I'd like to introduce a new client. This is Nick Reed. He has a new project he's working on, and I'd like you to work on the design part of his project."

Jan was so excited she was shaking. She couldn't believe it; she had been assigned to a special project and a new client. She couldn't wait to tell Ben and Chrissie, and she knew she would have to call her mom and dad.

"Yes, Mr. Bentley, I will do my best. It is very nice to meet you, Mr. Reed, and I look forward to working with you on your project."

"I am quite sure I will enjoy working with you as well."

Jan left the office and returned to her office. She immediately called Ben and Chrissie; they were all excited for her. As they talked, they made plans to go bowling and eat pizza to celebrate the new assignment.

After work, the three met at the front door and walked to the parking lot together. They were laughing and talking like giddy teenagers.

"I'm going home to change my clothes and call Mom and Dad. I'll meet you at the Golden Lanes in thirty minutes."

"Okay, see you there," Ben and Chrissie yelled.

Jan hurried home, grabbed the phone, and called her mom. "Mom, guess what? I have been assigned to a new client on a special project. Ben, Chrissie, and I are going bowling and eat pizza to celebrate."

"Oh, honey, I am so proud of you! I am also glad that you have new friends that you are close to. I'll tell your dad when he gets home. He will be so excited."

"Love you, Mom! I better get my clothes changed and run. Ben and Chrissie are waiting for me. I will talk to you later."

Jan got ready and met her friends at the bowling lanes. They were having a really great time. As it got later, the three decided to call it a night and see each other the next day at work.

Morning came quickly, and Jan returned to work, meeting up with her friends. While she was working on a design, she heard a tap on her door. "Come in."

"Good morning, Jan!" It was Nick Reed.

"I am so surprised. I guess you want to get started right away on your design. Can you tell me what kind of a project we are working on?"

"Yes, I would like to get started."

They got busy as Nick explained the project to Jan. She drew a few ideas and carefully measured as he described the layout. "I'm getting kind of hungry. What do you say I get us some lunch and bring it back so we can keep working?"

"Well, I guess that would be okay."

"I know a great little deli around the corner. I will be right back."

Jan called Ben and Chrissie. "Hey, I am going to work through lunch on this new project. I'll see you guys tonight after work."

Nick returned with lunch, and they visited while they ate. "I like to get to know the people I work with. Tell me about yourself, Jan."

"Oh, there's not much to tell. I've only been here six months. I have two great friends. We are real close, and I love my job."

They continued working throughout the afternoon. Jan was getting pretty tired. Nick looked at his watch. "Oh my, it's almost four. I have a plane to catch. I'll be out of town a couple of days. I will call when I get back and see how it's coming along."

"That's great. It will give me time to get a good idea down on paper."

Nick left the office. Jan gave a sigh. She was exhausted. She just wanted some quiet time, to not have to think. She slowly gathered her things and got ready to leave for the day.

Jan and her friends met at the front and walked to the parking lot. "Let's go to the buffet around the corner and eat, then we can go to my house for some television and relaxing. I am exhausted."

"That sounds like a good idea!"

"Yeah, let's go!"

As they grouped around the buffet and enjoyed their meal, Chrissie asked, "So what is this new client like?"

"He is real cute, very businesslike and polite."

"Oh, what is the business going on in *that* office?" They all laughed.

After dinner, they returned to Jan's to watch television and relax. It was another great evening for the threesome. When the evening got late, they all called it a night and parted for their own homes.

Morning came quickly once again for Jan. She prepared for work and drove to her job. There in the parking lot was Ben and Chrissie, playfully arguing as they usually did. They entered the building together and got on the elevator to the third floor. When they arrived at Jan's office, she opened the door, and much to her surprise, a huge bouquet of roses sat on her desk. All three were amazed and astonished.

"Oh my, what is this?" Looking at the card, Jan said, "It's from Nick Reed." She opened the card. It read, "Will you have dinner with me on Friday?" Jan was so shocked and really didn't know what to think, yet she felt excited inside. It was all she could think about through the day, and it was two days until Friday.

After work, Jan met up with her friends in the parking lot like usual. "How about sandwiches and salads at my house, guys? I am washed out!" Jan asked her friends.

"We know. You have your mind on Nick, and your mind is fogged up," Ben said, laughing at Jan.

"We'll meet you at your house, Jan. I have chips, salad, and a pie to contribute for dinner," added Chrissie.

Jan drove on home, tired from the long day and the long drive home, which wasn't that long but seemed to be because her mind was on Nick. Before she knew it, she had driven clear across town, and now she had to turn around and drive all the way home.

As she pulled in her driveway, there sat her friends waiting for her. "Jan, where have you been? We were getting worried."

Laughing about her mishap, she said, "You will never believe it. I just kept driving and missed my turn and ended up on the other side of town."

All three laughed as they entered the house and busily prepared the sandwich supper they had planned. The three were very close, and they could pick up on each other's moods. They enjoyed a joyful evening of fellowship together, but it was getting late, and before long, it was time to go their separate ways for the evening.

"Jan, we love you and care about you! *Please* be careful and take this slow. Don't rush a relationship with this man. You don't know anything about him," Chrissie added as they were leaving.

"I promise, I will be careful!" Jan laughed.

The next day, at work, Jan went through the motions of her job. Lunch in the break room with her friends was a welcome release for Jan as she always enjoyed the time with her friends. Friday finally arrived, and it was the day of her dinner date with Nick. She didn't know how to feel; she was excited but nervous as well. She went through the day, and late in the afternoon, she heard a tap on the door. She looked up to find Nick standing there at her door. "Hi! Are you joining me for dinner tonight?" he asked.

Jan nodded her head. "Yes, I plan to," she answered.

"I have a meeting with Mr. Bentley, then I'll be back, and we can leave from here," suggested Nick.

Jan called Chrissie and informed her of the evenings plan, and again Chrissie advised Jan to go slow.

A while later, Nick returned and asked if Jan was ready to leave for their dinner date. They left together. Nick opened his car door and helped Jan into the car. He drove to a nice small restaurant, where they enjoyed a nice dinner and visited, telling each other about themselves. It was a very comfortable dinner for the both of them. It was getting late, and when they realized the time, it was closing time at the restaurant, so Nick drove Jan back to her car.

"I would like to see you again," stated Nick.

"That would be nice," answered Jan.

Nick leaned over and gave Jan a light soft kiss on the cheek and said good night. Jan got out of his car and got in her car to go home.

Days turned into weeks, Jan continued to spend time with her friends. They went shopping, bowling, played games, and just hung out at each other's houses. They went to church on Sundays and out to eat. They had a great time together, but Jan's mind kept reflecting back to her date with Nick.

CHAPTER 10

In the coming months, Jan continued her close relationship with Ben and Chrissie, and when Nick would come to town, Jan would go out with him. She seemed to be getting closer to him and anxiously waited for him to come to town.

Many times, Ben and Chrissie expressed their concerns that Jan really knew nothing about him and to be very careful. Jan would laugh it off, and they would continue hanging out.

The early spring brought in the birth of new plant life, and the weather was comfortable. Everything was going beautifully in Jan's life. Her job was going great; she had amazing friends to fellowship with, and most of all, she was falling in love.

As spring turned into summer, Nick was continually showing a deeper, fonder side of himself. They spent more time together than usual. Jan felt that things were great between them, but she couldn't get Nick to talk about his family or his past. She just didn't put much thought into it when he wouldn't open up.

Ten months after meeting Nick, he called Jan at work one day out of the blue. "Hello, sweetheart, I have a big surprise. I will be there when you get off work. I will see you soon!"

"What is the surprise I can't wait to know?"

"Now, now, be patient. I will be there soon."

Jan was giddy all afternoon. When she took her break, she told Ben and Chrissie all about the phone call. They were a little leery about the sudden arrival and surprise.

The workday came to an end, and Jan gathered her things and headed for the elevator, where she met up with Ben and Chrissie. As they entered the parking garage, there stood Nick.

They exchanged greetings; Nick leaned over and gave Jan a kiss on the cheek. After a few minutes of small talk, Jan and Nick left in his car. He drove to a very nice restaurant. They went in and were seated.

"Okay! What is the big surprise? I have been on pins and needles all day. Tell me! What is it?" In her mind, she was thinking, maybe now he will share some things about his life.

"You sure are a bubbly little thing!" Laughing and reaching into his pocket, he gets down on one knee beside her. "Will you marry me?" he said, opening the small box for her to see.

"Oh yes, yes! I will!" She was shocked and surprised all at the same time, and the tears were streaming down her cheeks. This was the happiest moment of all for her.

"I have to go back out of town in the morning, but I promise when I return, I will begin to help with planning our very special day. Let's go celebrate and forget everything else!"

Jan squealed with excitement. She grabbed her purse and keys, and they headed out the door. They went to their favorite restaurant and had a gourmet dinner. Jan was floating on the clouds. Nothing else had ever made such an impression on her; she was in love and couldn't believe how happy she was. She floated through the night.

The next morning, as the sun came through her bedroom window, she couldn't stop looking at the ring on her finger. She just could not believe that it was really true. She grabbed the phone and called her mom.

"Mom! Nick proposed last night! I said yes!" She was screaming and laughing at the same time.

"Oh my goodness, Jan! I am so happy for you. Have you set a date yet?"

"No, he had to leave town again this morning, but when he gets back, we will start making plans."

"Well, I would love to help with your plans."

"Oh, of course. I need your help!"

"Wait until your father hears the news. This is absolutely wonderful!"

"I have to get to work, so I will talk to you later. Love you, Mom."

Jan started her day still floating. As soon as she met up with Ben and Chrissie, she could hardly contain herself. She had to share her news with them; she showed them her ring and asked for their help planning the wedding. They exchanged glances, and Jan noticed their look. "I know what you two are thinking. I just want you to be happy for me!"

"Honey, we are happy for you. We are just concerned. You have only been seeing him such a short time and still don't know anything about him."

"You know we are here for you whatever you need!"

"Great! Let's get together tonight for sandwiches or pizza at my house and discuss some plans."

Laughing and all giddy, they all went into the building to start their prospective workday.

Everyone was busy throughout the day. Jan couldn't stop looking at her ring, and then she would look at the phone, but it never rang. She passed it off as Nick probably working and being too busy. He would call when he could. That evening, the three friends gathered together and went to Jan's house. They agreed on ordering a pizza. All giggling together, they enjoyed each other's company and had a great time discussing a few ideas for the wedding and reception. As the night drew to an end, Ben and Chrissie left to go home. Jan looked at the clock. She thought, *How strange. No phone call.* She proceeded to get ready for bed.

As the days went by, she was still on a cloud. The weekend was quickly approaching. Jan's parents arrived for a surprise visit to see what they could do to help out. The weekend flew by, but they had started making plans and hired a wedding planner. It was time to start a new workweek. Jan was starting to feel down. Not one single call from Nick. She was starting to worry as the week dragged on. She didn't even know how to get ahold of him.

As Jan went through her week, she had times of crying and some depression; she didn't want to say anything to anyone. She was afraid they might be right about their suspicions. She continued to spend as much time with her friends as she could, and they discussed plans as if nothing were wrong.

On Friday evening, they walked out to the parking lot. As Jan got closer to her car, there he stood like a dream. Jan ran to him almost in tears. "I missed you. You didn't call, and I was so worried!"

"I had to be out of the country, and I didn't have any chances to call. I'm sorry. I didn't mean to make you worry."

They went out to eat and discuss some of the plans that Jan, her friends, and parents had made. Nick was very agreeable with all the plans. "It will be hard for me to do a lot as much as I have to be gone, but whatever you choose to do will be okay with me. Maybe your parents and Ben and Chrissie can help more."

"Everyone is so willing to help, but I wish you were not going to be gone so much."

"It will be okay. After we are married, you can travel with me. Right now, it is all in the planning stages, and I have to be on-site."

Jan believed him and told herself she just needed to be patient and everything would work out.

Nick was in town longer this time. So many of the wedding plans were taken care of. Everything was back to normal. Jan was so happy and back into the swing of things. She feared every day she saw Nick would be the day he would say he was leaving again. She tried to just put it out of her mind and enjoy having him around.

One day at work, several of her designs were finished, so she spent several hours in the laminating department. She didn't care for this part of her job, yet she had to spend several hours at times to complete her designs.

Chrissie was on the floor where Jan's office was and noticed she was out of her office, so she started looking for her. As Chrissie was walking down the hallway, she heard shouting. It sounded like Nick and her boss. She went into the office next to where they were shouting and listened.

"What do you mean by getting married? Are you crazy? With all this going on, this is impossible! How much does she know?"

"You don't have to worry about a thing. I am being very careful!"

"Don't you see the mess this causes? I will end up having to clean up the mess, like all the other times!"

"You just stay out of this. I can handle everything, and nothing will go wrong!"

Chrissie didn't understand the problem, but she became very frightened for Jan; she didn't know whether to tell her or not and how she could tell her.

Chrissie ran into Ben, so she told him everything she heard. "What do you think is going on? What should we do? I am so afraid for Jan."

"No matter what we do, we have to protect Jan. We must tell her!"

After work, the three met up to walk to the parking lot like they normally did. Chrissie got the nerve to say something. "Jan, let's all go to my house and have a sandwich and snacks, I think we need to talk."

Jan looked at Chrissie, very curious about her tone of voice.

"Yeah, great. Maybe even some games to help us relax. I spent the afternoon laminating designs."

The three drove to Chrissie's. When they arrived, they were all laughing and happy to be together. They prepared drinks, sandwiches, chips, and other finger food out of the fridge. As they sat down to eat, still laughing and playing with each other, Chrissie's demeanor changed.

"Jan, I have to tell you something. It's hard to do, and I don't want you to get upset with Ben or me."

Ben added, "It's important we discuss this."

"Okay, guys, it sounds important. What's going on?" Jan asked, very curious now.

Chrissie began telling Jan what she had heard earlier that afternoon. As she went on, Jan became shocked. "What do you think is going on?"

"I couldn't piece it together or make any sense of the whole conversation." Chrissie proceeded, "Ben and I care about you, and maybe you should wait awhile on the wedding until you find out what is going on."

"I will confront Nick and ask what is going on. I'll ask why our marriage would interfere in my boss's plans."

"Do you really think that is a wise thing to do? We don't know what's going on, and you could get hurt."

The evening was drawing to a close, and Jan decided she needed to get home as she hadn't heard from Nick all day.

She went on home and started getting ready for bed. The phone rang. It was Nick! Jan was remembering what Ben and Chrissie had told her. She wanted to trust Nick and ask him about the argument Chrissie had overheard but decided it was probably better to wait.

"I called to let you know I am flying out in the morning and I will be gone for over a week. I am sorry. I won't be much help with the wedding plans, after all."

"That's okay. I think a lot of it is done. Mom, Ben, and Chrissie have helped a lot!"

"I'll see you when I get back. Love you!"

"Love you!"

As the phone clicked, she felt betrayed and lost, maybe even a little frightened. She wasn't sure what to do next.

Jan went through the following week wearing a mask so as to not let anyone see how she was hurting or how confused she was about her relationship with Nick. She continued to go through the motions with making her wedding plans, yet she was wondering if it would end up being canceled. She spent as much time with Ben and Chrissie as she could. They cheered her up, and she could forget the worries on her mind.

On Friday, Jan went to the employee lounge, where Ben and Chrissie spent lunch. The three joked and teased each other playfully so they could relax some before finishing up their day. Jan popped up with the spur-of-the-moment idea. "Hey guys, let's order in tonight and watch movies at my house."

Ben cut in, "How about bowling and pizza at the Golden Lanes?"

"Great idea!" Chrissie and Jan exclaimed at the same time. "We could meet about seven."

So the final decision was agreed upon. Jan left the lounge to return to her work. When she entered her office, there, to her surprise, were a dozen long-stemmed red roses with a card. "Be home soon. Love you, Nick." At least he hadn't totally forgotten about her. Smiling to herself, she continued with her work. Jan went home right after work to change clothes and was off to the bowling alley. Ben and Chrissie had arrived ahead of her.

They ordered pizza and began to bowl, laughing and trying to see who could outbowl the other. They had a great time. The evening spilled right by. They were having so much fun together and were so relaxed after a long workweek. The manager announced that it was time to finish up; they were getting ready to close.

"My, I sure didn't know it was getting to be that late already. I have been enjoying tonight so much and lost track of time. I am so glad that we decided on bowling!" Jan was so full of joy.

They all left the alley to go home. They were very tired. It was a good kind of tired for a change. Jan got home and was ready for bed. She didn't have any trouble falling asleep.

As the sun started coming through the window early the next morning, she was awakened by the doorbell. She put on her robe and went to the door. There stood Nick. What a surprise! Jan opened the door and let him in. They went into the kitchen, where Jan started coffee and breakfast. "How was your trip?" she asked.

"It was okay. I think we have it about settled. I am staying here now until after our wedding. I haven't been much help, but I plan to change that."

"That's great!" Jan tried to act convinced and happy, but she thought it would only be a matter of time until she would see how true that would actually be.

The days led into weeks and the weeks into one month then two. Nick was staying in town; there was no mention of leaving town. Nick was busy helping with the wedding plans. He was so in love with Jan, and he wanted the best for her. During the outings with Ben and Chrissie he welcomed their friendship as the four of them were the best of friends; he didn't mind the closeness between them and Jan.

It came down to the week before the wedding; Jan's parents came and stayed to be there to help with last-minute arrangements. Jan's boss let her have the week off. Everything was going absolutely perfect. Jan thought to herself that maybe what Chrissie had heard was just a misunderstanding. Everything was just perfect. She was so happy.

The day of the rehearsal and rehearsal dinner had arrived; Jan was floating in the clouds. She could hardly sleep that night. The next day, she was going to be married, and her name would be Mrs. Nick Reed. She couldn't be happier.

The morning sun woke her, and she beamed as she saw her wedding dress hanging there just waiting for the day's event. Jan crawled out of bed and joined her parents for breakfast and coffee, laughing and being giddy.

"You know, this is the last day you will be our little girl. After today you will be a married woman," Jan's father stated almost tearfully.

"Now let's not get emotional, or we will never get through the day." Jan laughed. They busily cleaned up things and started getting ready to go to the church. Nothing entered into their thoughts outside of the day's events. Honeymoon bags were packed. Final arrangements of the cleanup and bringing everything back to Jan's had been made. It was time to leave for the church. Everyone was getting nervous and anxious.

The drive seemed to take forever. The church parking lot was already full of cars. They could hear the organ playing. Jan and her father went into the waiting area. Corene was escorted down the aisle to the front of the church. As she looked about the beautifully decorated church and all the people she knew, family and friends from home and new friends Jan had met since she moved here, the one thing she noticed was that there were only a few of Nick's family and friends. She didn't put much thought into it as she knew that Jan had told her Nick didn't have family.

Everyone stood at the front of the church at the altar. The organ started playing the wedding march; it was now time for Jan and her father to make that walk down the aisle. There she was on her father's arm, walking into a different life. Corene was in a daze as Jan and Nick went through the ceremony, pledging their love for each other. Corene kept praying that Jan would be happy and have the life she wanted. The ceremony was beautiful, and Jan was such a lovely bride.

As everyone went into the reception hall following the ceremony, they were all drawn aback. It was absolutely breathtaking; the cake was beautiful, and the gift table was full of beautifully wrapped gifts. It was a beautiful day, almost like a dream.

Everyone seemed to have a great time during the festivities. Corene looked around at how happy everyone was. *So why do I feel so strange about things?* she thought to herself. As people began to leave, Jan and Nick went to change and prepare to leave for the airport for their honeymoon.

Nick and Jan came out to say good-bye to the guests and Ken and Corene.

"Have a safe trip and have loads of fun. Come see us when you can! Nick, please take care of our daughter," Ken replied with a lump in his throat.

The newlyweds turned and went to the car and drove off. Ken and Corene busied themselves gathering up items, cleaning up, taking all the decorations down, and loading the car. Ben and Chrissie stayed to help and volunteered to take everything to Jan's house. It took the rest of the afternoon to get it all cleaned up.

After arriving at Jan's, everyone was carrying items in the house.

"When are you going back home?" Ben asked Corene.

"Not until sometime tomorrow. It will give us time to clean up and put things away so that when they get home, they don't have a mess to deal with."

"Something is bothering you, isn't it, Mama?" asked Chrissie.

"No, I'm just a little tired from all the excitement. I will be fine when reality sets in. You know Jan has been through a lot."

Ben gave Corene a hug, then did the same with Ken. "Well, we both have to work tomorrow, and it has been a long day, so you have a safe trip home tomorrow. Hope to see you again soon."

"Bye for now. Love you both!" Corene added.

Ben and Chrissie left. It was just Ken and Corene getting things taken care of.

"Honey, what's wrong? You have been in another world all day. You might tell everyone else you are tired, but I know something is bothering you!"

"No, I really am tired, and I guess maybe I am worried about Jan," answered Corene.

They went to bed after doing as much as they could, both of them exhausted from such a long day. The night passed quickly, and soon they were up preparing breakfast. Corene was still quiet and did not want to worry Ken, so she kept her feelings to herself.

They busied themselves cleaning up and putting things away in an organized manner so Jan could care for them on her return. It was now time for them to head back home.

CHAPTER 11

The next two weeks went by very quickly. The honeymoon was terrific. Nick and Jan had a great hotel room. Breakfast was brought to their room every morning. They swam in the pool and sat on the beach and took plane rides, tours. It was every woman's dream come true.

Back home, Ben and Chrissie continued to work, yet they felt a coldness about the office. They tried to listen to coworkers at lunch and breaks to determine the reason for the drop in morale. Nothing came to give them any understanding. They speculated it had to do with Nick and Jan getting married but couldn't come up with anything conclusive.

Ken and Corene were back home and going about their daily routine, but they were also missing Jan. They were hoping that everything was going well for her and Nick. Corene was still feeling an uneasiness, though she could not determine why. Worry just seemed to linger day in and day out.

It was finally time for Nick and Jan to return home. As they boarded the plane to fly home, they took one last look. They both felt saddened as the two weeks had been glorious for both of them.

They finally arrived home after a long flight. They found their car and drove home. As Nick unloaded the car, Jan called her mom. "Hi, Mom, we are home!"

"Hello! I am so glad you called! Did you have a good time?"

"Oh man! Everything was amazing. We had such a terrific time. We hated to leave." After talking for a few minutes, Jan told her mom she needed to call Ben and Chrissie and help Nick unpack. Jan made her calls to Ben and Chrissie, then started helping Nick unpack. They walked into the spare bedroom. Everything from the wedding and the reception was there. Corene had put everything in as much order as she could, so it wasn't difficult to get everything put away and taken care of.

After, Nick and Jan collapsed on the couch in front of the television. They were exhausted, and with all the excitement, they just needed to rest.

Jan turned to Nick. "Are you hungry, sweetheart?"

"I could eat a bite. Let's check the fridge."

Off to the kitchen they went to fix something. They found some things to throw together for sandwiches. Laughing and playing around, they realized how happy and in love they were.

"Jan, you are everything to me. I am so glad we found each other. I want to spend my whole life proving my love for you."

"I love you so much!"

After they finished eating, they decided to take showers and get ready for bed as tomorrow was the first day of the rest of their life. Being so tired, they both fell asleep very quickly. The next morning, Nick and Jan rose and fixed breakfast and coffee. As they sat down to eat, they were both thinking the same thing.

"You know, honey, in a few days it will be time to get back to work. I will have to start going out of town again."

"I know. I guess I will have to get used to the idea and adjust to it."

"I sure hope that everything will be okay and that we can accept each other's lives."

Jan knew that the day would come, but she was going to work harder at her job, and besides, she had Ben and Chrissie.

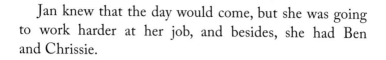

They continued the rest of their honeymoon time enjoying things they wanted to do. Finally, they went back to work. Everyone was glad to see Jan, and when she saw Ben and Chrissie, they hugged and laughed.

"It is so good to see you. I am glad you are back!" Chrissie burst out.

"Me too!"

They went on break together and ate lunch just like nothing had happened or changed. Getting back to work was not a problem for Jan. She started right where she left off.

The days went by; they led into weeks and then into one month, then two. Nick had not left town since they got back. One night as they were eating supper, Jan asked, "I'm not complaining, but you haven't left town. What happened?"

"They don't need me to go out of town for a while, which I am so glad for."

Everything was still good after six months; their love was still going strong. One afternoon, as Jan was working, she heard a knock at the door. It was Nick. He walked into the office.

"Honey, I have to go home and pack. I need to fly out tonight!"

"Okay, I guess I can share you. I have had you to myself this long, and I promised you I would be okay with this."

"You're the best, sweetie!"

Out the door he went. When they took a break, Ben and Chrissie came into Jan's office. "Hey guys, want to go for pizza tonight? Nick is leaving town tonight."

"That's a great idea! Let's go right after work. I'm already starving!"

Ben looked at her closely. "Are you okay with Nick leaving town?"

"Yeah, I am good. I don't like it, but it is what it is." All three laughed all giddy-like.

Each day went by; Jan was okay but curious about his absence. Their life together was good. Time had flown by fast. It was time to celebrate their first anniversary. Jan was excited as Nick had planned a night out to remember.

Nick and Jan had been married eighteen months, Nick was out of town. Jan was working, but lately, she was very tired and started feeling feverish. She got up and started to go get a drink of water. As she entered the hallway, she felt weak, and her eyes turned dark. She passed out and fell to the floor.

Everyone ran to her side. One secretary called the ambulance, and Mr. Brent ran out. "I will call Nick!"

The ambulance arrived. They worked on Jan and put her on a gurney and rushed her to the hospital. Ben and Chrissie rushed to the hospital. On the way, they called Ken and Corene to let them know.

"What happened? Is she okay? Please stay with her and call us the minute you find something out!"

When Jan woke up, Nick was holding her hand. "Oh, baby, you are awake. They took some tests, and they will tell us something as soon as they get the results. What happened?"

"I didn't feel well, felt feverish, so I was going to get a drink of water. How long have I been out?"

"I don't think very long. Maybe a couple of hours. Ben and Chrissie are here."

"We called your mom and dad, so I better call them and let them know you are okay."

Ben and Chrissie left the room to call Jan's parents.

"Hi, Corene, Jan is awake now, and she is okay. They took some tests and will tell us something as soon as they can. Nick is with her now, and she said she will call you as soon as she finds out what happened."

"Thank you so much. Just please take care of her!"

"Oh, we will. Don't worry about that!"

Ben and Chrissie went back into the room. The doctor came in shortly after that.

"Congratulations, Mr. and Mrs. Reed! You are six weeks pregnant, and that is what caused you to get feverish and weak and pass out. We will keep you overnight. You are still a little anemic, so tomorrow when you go home, I will give you some prescriptions for vitamins and iron."

Nick jumped up. Jan's eyes got as big as dollars. Ben and Chrissie shrieked with joy.

"Baby? Oh my gosh, a baby!" Nick started crying and hugging Jan.

"I can't believe this. I just never even thought about a baby!" Jan was crying as well. "Hand me the phone please. I need to call my parents!" Crying, she dialed the number. "Hello, Mom! I am doing okay except for a small problem. Mom, I'm pregnant!"

"We're going to be grandparents? wow! Oh, I'm so happy for you!"

"Now we can plan a baby shower!" Chrissie smiled.

The next day, Jan was released to go home. Nick was there to take his wife home. Everyone knew that the news would fly all over in her hometown and her job, and they were not wrong. Jan started receiving cards and baby gifts. Nick and Jan started discussing turning the small bedroom into the nursery. Nick was so excited about having a baby.

"I'm going to get started on fixing it into the nursery. I think we should leave the twin bed in there, in case there are nights one of us needs to stay with the baby."

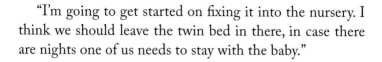

Jan was feeling better and went back to work on that following Monday. Everyone was hugging her and glad to see her. Everyone was talking about a big baby shower. She was so happy. It was now close to their second anniversary. She was proud how great things had been.

That next weekend, Ken and Corene went to see Nick and Jan. When they arrived, they were welcomed happily by the couple.

"Come, look at the nursery!" Nick said, excited. They all went upstairs and walked into the small bedroom.

"Oh, Nick, it's beautiful. You have done an excellent job!"

"Thank you, I'm glad you like it. We have been getting baby things from everywhere, and everyone is talking about a baby shower!"

"I should get together with Ben and Chrissie and help with it. There are several people from home that want to come."

Within a month, the baby shower was planned to be held at the church they attended. Many people came carrying beautifully wrapped gifts. Several people brought colorfully decorated refreshments. Games were organized. The celebration was enjoyed by everyone, by so many friends and relatives. Everything was just lovely.

When the party was over, Ken and Corene helped Nick and Jan take everything home and get some kind of order in the nursery.

"The nursery is complete. Now all we need is the baby to come home!" Corene stated, and everyone laughed.

Jan was starting to feel big and not a very lovable person. Nick was good about cheering her up and keeping her spirits up. Nick was holding her close and being very sweet as well as protective. The phone rang.

"I'll get it, sweetheart, and you rest," Nick said very lovingly.

She could hardly hear what was being said, and then Nick returned to the room. "Babe, it was ole Brent. I told him I'd come to the office. He's mad about something. Honey, why don't you take a shower and go to bed. I love you, and I'll be back as quick as I can."

"Okay, that's a good idea. I am so tired."

Nick drove across town to Brent's Designs to see what the problem was. As he got off the elevator, he was met by Brent.

"Just what in the devil do you think you are doing?"

"I don't understand."

"You know what we are into. No, you go get married and now a baby? Mr. Happy Family Man! You take care of this mess, and I mean now! Before that baby comes!"

"Now wait a minute, this is my family you are talking about, and you just can't dismiss what I want in my life—"

"Either you get it done, or I will. It's not like you are so innocent. Do you want to spend the rest of your life in jail? Well, I don't!"

Nick turned and left, very angry and upset about the conversation. He couldn't go home to Jan right now with this on his mind. He drove around a while and then stopped at a bar for a drink. After a couple of drinks, he headed home. *Jan should be asleep, and I won't have to deal with this tonight*, he thought.

He arrived home and quietly went up to the bedroom. As he walked past the nursery, he stopped; a tear ran down his cheek. *How could this be happening?* he thought. He quietly got ready for bed and slid in beside Jan. She was so tired, and she didn't deserve what was coming up.

The next morning, he went to the kitchen. Jan greeted him. She had breakfast and coffee ready, and she was smiling from ear to ear.

"Well, how did your meeting go last night?"

"He can't find some designs. Supposed to be finalized soon, and he thinks I left them in South America!"

"Does this mean you will be leaving again?"

"Oh, I hope not. I want to be here when the baby comes!"

The next few days were very tense for Nick; he went to talk with Mr. Brent about him just taking his family and leaving to get out of his situation, but he was told how it would never work, and where would he go?

"I have a plan, and you just go along with it. We can send you out of the country, and then we can start all over!"

"No, I just want out!"

"You don't have any say. There is only one way out!"

Nick went home before Jan got home. When she walked in, she was very surprised to see him.

"Let's go out to eat tonight!"

"Okay, that sounds good."

He wanted to make it the best night ever. "Do you know how much I love you?"

"Yes, I do. What's wrong? You seem so stressed and upset. I want to help you. I don't like seeing you this way!"

They drove around a while and returned home afterward. While resting in front of the television, the phone rang. "I'll get it, babe!"

"Yes, I'll get her."

"Honey, it's for you."

Jan went to the phone and talked for a few minutes and returned to Nick. "I have to go to the office. Mr. Brent is real upset. It must be the same designs he was after you about. Do you want to go with me?"

"No, I have some work in my briefcase I just have to have done by tomorrow. You go ahead."

Jan drove to her office. Mr. Brent met her and started yelling at her about the missing designs. "I don't have to remind you this could cost our company millions of dollars if we do not meet these requirements and very soon."

"I understand. I will look for them right now!"

Going into her office, she began going through her files. After looking through the last six months of files, she found the folder. When she pulled it out, it was empty. Tears began to run down her face. She knew she was going to lose her job now. She took the empty folder to Mr. Brent. He was so furious. He just sent her home.

"Tomorrow we will comb the files good and see what we can do to fix this problem."

Jan left to return home. There, as she turned down her street, fire trucks and police blocked her street. As she got closer, she saw it was her house. She jumped out of her car, yelling, crying, "Nick, Nick, Nick! My husband! Where is he?"

The police grabbed her. "You can't go in there!"

Then she saw two men pushing a gurney toward her with a black zippered bag on top. She started screaming even worse. She was weak, and she dropped to her knees and passed out.

She woke up the next morning with Ben and Chrissie standing by her bed. She asked them with tears rolling down her cheeks, "What happened?"

"You don't remember? We have called your mom and dad. They are on their way."

"Is Nick gone? How did the fire start?"

"Honey, just rest. Wait until your parents get here, and they can talk to you."

Jan fell back to sleep. She started dreaming she was home with Nick and her baby and they were happy.

Jan would wake up jerking, screaming and calling out Nick's name. The nurses would come in and talk to her to calm her down. "Honey, you must stay calm. It's not good for you or the baby."

"I know! Why won't anyone tell me anything? Where is my husband?"

The doctor came in to check Jan and the baby. "Mrs. Reed, I am going to give you a light sedative. You need to rest, and your blood pressure is high." He administered the sedative through her IV, and soon she fell asleep. The doctor continued to monitor her blood pressure; once she was stable, he left the room.

Police officers were outside her door. "How soon can we question Mrs. Reed?"

Jan's doctor answered quietly, "I don't recommend it until her parents get here. She doesn't know what happened. She could lose the baby. I have her sedated right now. I have to get her blood pressure stabilized so she can rest."

"We will come back later when she's awake, but we must question her!"

A few hours later, Ken and Corene arrived at the hospital. The doctor met with them. "I am so glad you are here. No one has told her anything, and I have kept her sedated with a light sedative to keep her calm."

"How did all this happen?"

"Really, I don't know all the details, but the police have been here. I wouldn't let them question her until you got here."

"We are greatly thankful for everything you are doing! How's the baby?"

"We are keeping a close look and monitoring both your daughter and her baby."

As Ken and Corene went in to see Jan, Ben and Chrissie walked in. They all went in together. Corene went to sit by Jan and hold her hand.

"Mom, what is going on? I can't remember, and no one will tell me where Nick is!" Jan was very groggy and could hardly speak clearly. Before Corene could answer, the police walked in.

"Mrs. Reed, we know you are not feeling well, but we need to ask you some questions."

"What's going on? Where's Nick?"

"What do you remember about last night?"

"I think I went to the office. I remember seeing a fire, and that's it."

"Mrs. Reed, do you have keys to your office building?"

"No, Mr. Brent was there. He needed to talk to me about some designs."

"We talked to your boss. He was home, and he did not ask you to come to the office."

"I don't know. I can't remember!"

"Mrs. Reed, your husband is dead, and we have to place you under arrest!"

"What are you charging her with?" yelled Ken.

"Murder. We found designs hidden in the trunk under the spare tire. Mr. Brent identified them as the missing designs. The oven and heater pilots were turned off in the house, and the gas was still on. I suggest you find a good lawyer. When she is released from the hospital, she goes to jail."

Jan was hysterical. Everyone was crying. No one understood what was happening or even why.

"I'm going to get you a lawyer!" Ken was very angry. "Honey, you stay with Jan and try to keep her calmed down."

"Is there anything we can do to help?" Ben and Chrissie were just dumbfounded by everything.

"I guess just help keep Jan calmed down."

Jan was hysterical and upset. She was getting dizzy, and her head was spinning. Finally she passed out. The doctor came by to check on her. She was still sleeping, and the monitors showed she was doing okay. She continued to stay asleep for several hours. Corene prayed with Ben and Chrissie that everything would work out and they could take Jan through this.

After a few hours, Jan woke up screaming in pain and sweating profusely and went into a seizure. Corene ran out into the hall yelling for help. The nurses came running. The desk nurse called the doctor. He came running into the room. "Call the OR. We have to get her into surgery right away!"

Corene called Ken immediately. They rushed Jan out of the room to the OR. All were crying and very upset. Ken ran into the room. "What happened? Where is Jan?"

"They took her to the OR. I just know she's losing the baby."

"This will just be the end for her. She will not get over all this."

Two hours later, the doctor came into the room. His head hung down. "I'm so sorry. We couldn't save the baby. There was just too much trauma, and your daughter is in recovery. She is doing fine. She just doesn't know yet about the baby. Do you want to tell her, or do you want me to do it?"

"I think we should tell her. It's going to be hard on her, whoever tells her."

Jan was brought back to the room. She was very groggy. "Did you see her, Mom? I think I'll name her Nickie!" Jan dozed off to sleep.

"You rest now, dear." Corene was crying. "How are we going to tell her?"

"This is just a nightmare! How could all this have happened?" Ken was so angry. "I got her a lawyer, so I pray it will be okay."

Jan slept all night. She awoke early. "I feel so much better this morning. When can I see my baby?"

"Honey, I don't know how to say this easy. Jan, the baby did not make it. The doctor said there was just too much trauma. He worked on her, but it just did no good." She was crying as she told Jan the news.

Jan's face froze. Her eyes went lifeless, and she didn't say one word, just gave them a blank stare. The doctor came in to see how she was doing. "I've seen this before. It's a very deep depression. I don't want to give her anymore meds than what I have already given her for now."

Jan closed her eyes. Tears ran down her cheeks. Ken kissed her forehead and held her. Jan was lifeless. Ben and Chrissie talked to her about happy things. There was no reaction from Jan at all.

"We need to go now, but we will both be back tomorrow," Ben informed Ken and Corene.

As nightfall came, Jan had not eaten all day; she just slept. Ken and Corene slept by her bedside. The next day came. It was the same, so was the next day and the day after that. It was time to release Jan from the hospital. There was nothing more they could do for her.

Ken and Corene took Jan to the police department. The new lawyer also met them there. "Jan, honey, this is David Albright, your attorney. He is going to help you through this."

"The grand jury indicted her, so now we go to arraignment. I will try to get bail."

Jan was still frozen with a lifeless stare, showing no reaction to anything going on around her.

Ken and Corene waited outside the courtroom until David came out. "Where is Jan? How much is the bail?" Ken excitedly asked.

"I'm sorry, Ken, they want to hold her. She has no ties, her husband is dead, her home burned down, no job, and now her baby is dead. They feel she will flee.

Ken and Corene stayed with Ben and Chrissie as the trial was to soon begin. Days led into weeks, weeks into months. The trial started. It was not going well. Jan had no energy to help with her own defense and still showed no reaction to what was being said.

Ken and Corene were in the courtroom every day, along with Ben and Chrissie. It was a very devastating ordeal for them all. They could hardly believe the things being said about Nick and Jan.

After two long months of the long, drawn-out trial, it was over. The jury was out. Everyone was tense except for Jan. She just sat there listless. When the jury came in, they found Jan guilty of the murder of Nick Reed, her husband. They sentenced her to ten years in the state penitentiary. Corene passed out and dropped to the floor. No one could believe it.

Chapter 12

Ken and Corene went to visit Jan every day, their tears chasing each drop one after the other. "Dad, Mom, I love you very much, and I am so lucky to have both of you to support me through all this, but it's only torture for both of you. You can't do anything anymore. It's over. Let it go. Let me go and go on with your lives!"

"Don't be silly. You are our life, and we don't want to move on without you. We will fight to prove your innocence."

"You can't see me every day. When they move me, my life is over. I've lost everything except you guys and Ben and Chrissie."

It wasn't long until Jan was transferred to what was going to be her new home and the new life she would have to adapt to for the next ten years. It was five hundred miles away from Ken and Corene, so they wouldn't be coming too often. Ben and Chrissie had to work, so she probably wouldn't see too much of them either. Tears slowly ran down her cheeks. She was all alone again; she had lost her life and everyone in it.

As she walked into her cell and looked around, she thought to herself, *Now toughen up! Just don't remember!* Time passed, one day after another. Jan was assigned enough positions to keep her busy all day, so she didn't have time to ponder on anything, and by the time the lights were to be out, she was already asleep. She just didn't think. She just followed the rules and did her jobs and kept to herself.

On visiting days, her parents came, Ben and Chrissie too. They were good visits, and she was always so glad to see them. It gave her some hope for the future.

"I'm okay, really. I keep busy. I am so tired that I'm asleep before lights-out. I don't think. I just take one day at a time."

"That's not you. You were always happy and bubbly. We don't like seeing you like this."

"It's okay, don't worry!"

Jan had a calendar, and each day she marked the days off. Jan had some sense of peace. She knew she was safe; she wasn't going to let anyone into her world now.

The first year went by. Jan got along fairly well. It was very lonely for her, but she could stay out of trouble and not be reminded of the past.

The second year became a little rougher. The visits became fewer and fewer. The inmates seemed to be getting tougher and more rough-talking. At times she was fearful, and some of them started making fun of her, calling her Ms. Goody Two-shoes. She tried to stay away from the ones who tried to get close to her or made fun of her.

The letters she got from her parents and friends were encouraging and cheerful. As the time passed, she was forgetting the life before this awful nightmare happened.

In the third year, Jan got a letter. Her dad wasn't doing very well. He was continually working to prove Jan's innocence and talking to everyone he could. It was wearing on Ken in the worst way. The next letter she received, Ken had had a heart attack and was in the hospital, not doing very well. Jan cried knowing her problems had caused her father's illness. Corene stated in her letter she wasn't sure when they would be able to see her again.

Two months had passed since Jan received a letter from her mother. It was short. Ken had passed away; his heart hadn't been able to take anymore. Corene was not well either; she had been in the hospital as well.

Ben and Chrissie had come as much as they could. They wanted to keep it as quiet as they could because they were trying to help Jan as well, and they didn't want to lose their jobs. It was hard on them to see their friend all by herself, having lost everything.

When Jan had reached the halfway point of her sentence, she was so delighted, yet she didn't want to start making any plans either. She knew things could change in a heartbeat.

Ben, Chrissie, and Corene came to visit on visiting day. "Jan, I am going to make my will and leave everything to you, but Ben and Chrissie will have to be the executors until you get out."

"Mom, I don't want to talk about these things now, and I sure don't want to make any plans for the future until I know I have a future."

"Well, you will have a home and a living to get yourself started. I'm not feeling well, and I miss your dad and you so very much."

Jan continued to meet each day with a positive attitude. Letters from her mother helped, as well as letters from Ben and Chrissie.

Jan never got to see her mom again after that last visit. Ben and Chrissie came to visit and broke the sad news to her that her mom had passed away; they also told her that they were conducting the business with settling her estate for Jan.

"We will keep up the house until you get out and keep the accounts up-to-date so everything will be ready and waiting for you when you get out."

"Thank you so much for taking care of things and for being there for my parents through this whole ordeal. They needed someone on their side." Tears rolled down her face.

She lay in her bed gazing into the darkness. *Maybe now it is time to start thinking about what I will do after I get out of here,* she thought. *I'm not sure how things will be. I don't have anything to get out for.*

Each night the darkness engulfed her. She was feeling weaker, and her sorrow took over. She would become very confused, just not knowing where to turn. The intimidation was worse; some of the inmates started becoming physical with her, poking her, pushing her into walls and tripping her.

She went to the chapel and talked with the chaplain about her struggles and how her sorrow was taking over. He would comfort her the best he could, but he could see she was suffering inside and out, and he just knew she was going to become bitter and maybe even violent in some way.

A week later as she was ending her duties in the laundry, she walked out the door like she always did. Three inmates were standing there waiting for her, and they pushed her back in the laundry. They started slugging her. She fell to the floor. All three took turns stabbing her and cutting her hair and face. She couldn't see; the darkness began to engulf her with a distant light. She couldn't feel the pain of the stabbing; her mind took her back home, where she was with her parents. She lay in a pool of her own blood for what seemed like hours.

Her roommate went to look for her when it got late and she hadn't returned. She found Jan and ran for help. Jan was immediately rushed to the infirmary. She was barely alive, with all the cuts she received, no one knew how it was possible that she was still breathing. All the doctors and nurses began to work on her. They worked all night not knowing for sure what chances she had. Only time would tell. The chaplain called Ben and Chrissie to notify them of what had happened.

Ben and Chrissie drove to the institution where Jan was. They were allowed to stay with Jan and sit with her.

Jan was wrapped in dressings and bandages head to toe; she was unrecognizable. Tubes and pumps kept her alive. Day after day passed, Jan made no progress and no movements. Ben and Chrissie stayed right by her side.

"Oh, what a horrible thing this is."

"What a terrible way for an ending. None of this makes any sense."

After two weeks, Ben and Chrissie saw some movement; Jan was actually twitching and moving her fingers. The doctors examined her for a long time.

"Your friend is very strong. She is slowly pulling through. Now there may be other problems we have not noticed or found. I suggest you both pray and pray a lot."

Each day, she improved. After a week, she started moving her head and moving her lips to talk. As the wounds were healing, there were less and less bandages. Jan had deep cuts, so she would have a lot of scars.

After a month, Jan was starting to talk some. The authorities came in to try to interview her to find out who did this. Jan was not much help. She couldn't remember anything. All she knew was she was in pain.

Six months had passed. Jan was talking more, and no bandages were left. The doctors brought a mirror for her to see how well she had healed. Tears began to roll down her deformed face. "I look like a monster! I look horrible! Why didn't you let me die?"

"Young lady, you have been through a lot, but that does not mean it is the end of the world."

Therapy began to strengthen her muscles and got her walking on her own. It was very painful, but she did not give up. Each day she continued, determined to get herself back to her original health.

Once she was able to walk and talk, she was moved to a less populated part of the institution so she would not be attacked again and so she could get used to being around people again.

Ben and Chrissie continued to come and visit; they did everything they could to cheer her up. Eventually Jan smiled and laughed with them.

The authorities continued to question Jan. She just could not remember that night at all. She didn't want to remember, nor did she care who caused all the problems and almost killed her. Her attorney came to see her. He was very upset about what happened to her.

"You now need reconstructive surgery, and I am going to do what I can to see that you get it!"

"Just what good is that going to do? I look like a freak, and I will always be a freak!"

"No, not after you have these surgeries at the state's expense. You can have a life again once you are out of here."

After Jan and her lawyer had finished discussing the procedure he was about to attempt, Jan went back to her part of the building. She was escorted by a guard.

"You know, you have been a perfect inmate during your stay here. It just isn't fair what has happened to you. I just hope you can put your life back together."

"I don't know. Maybe someday. I've had to force myself to go from day to day, but every time I find happiness, something terrible happens to me, and I am back to square one."

"Things will change when you get out."

Jan settled down to rest. She started thinking about things and what she would do when she did get out. She fell asleep. She started dreaming. She saw a girl she didn't know. It was her. She was home and happy.

Ben and Chrissie came to visit the next visiting day. Jan was so happy to see them. "Guys, I love you both. I know it's hard to travel this far. I am so glad you two have stuck by me."

"We wouldn't have done any different. Remember, we are the Three Musketeers. We have to stick together."

"My lawyer was here. He's going to start a case against the state for them to do reconstructive surgery. I had a dream, and I saw a girl. I didn't know her, but she was so beautiful, then I realized it was me."

"See, things are turning out better, and good things are going to happen for you."

Jan smiled wanly, and Chrissie, wanting to lighten the mood, hurriedly changed topics. "On our way here, we saw a new restaurant that just opened. I think on our way back we will stop there to eat."

They continued their visit as long as they were allowed to. Jan was so happy her friends were there to be with her.

The escort guard walked with Jan back to her cell. Jan was feeling more happy and hopeful. She went fast asleep and rested well. Again she started to dream about a beautiful girl.

Ben and Chrissie had started the long drive back home. When they reached the new restaurant they had spotted, they decided to stop and eat some dinner. When they went in, they noticed it was extremely busy. The waitress led them to a corner booth. They looked over the menu and ordered. The wait was not too long. As they sipped their drinks, they talked and laughed, rejoicing over the changes in Jan. The waitress set the food down in front of them; it smelled so good. They gave a thankful prayer and began to eat.

"Ben, look over there in the corner booth across the building!"

"Who is that, Chrissie?"

"Am I blind? It looks just like Nick!"

"Can't be, the darkness of the room is making his looks different."

"Don't let him see us. If it is him, there could be problems."

"We have to find out if that's Nick, though."

The waitress came to the table. "Is there anything else I can get for you?"

"No, thank you, but can I ask you a something? Who is that couple over there in the corner? They look like someone we know, but we aren't sure."

"That is Mr. and Mrs. Thomas Harper. They deal in land development and real estate here in Cambridge. Are you all from around here?"

"No, we live about another four hours down the road."

They thanked the waitress and went on with their dinner and conversation.

"We have got to make sure that is Nick. It has been several years!" Chrissie said.

"He's going into the bathroom. I will go in and see if I can hear him talk so I can make sure whether or not it's him."

"Be careful! Don't let him see you. It could be dangerous for all of us."

Tom went into the men's room; Ben waited a few minutes and went in behind him. Ben was in luck; he slipped into an empty stall, and Mr. Harper never saw him. Someone else went into the restroom. Ben could not recognize the voice.

"Well, hello, Tom. I haven't seen you in ages. You been out of town again? How are you doing anyway?"

"Hey, Carl. Yeah, I just got back yesterday. We are good as a juicy Georgia peach."

Both men laughed as they headed for the door. Ben looked out of the stall; he was all alone. He slipped out of the restroom and looked to see where Tom had gone. Both of the men had returned to Tom's table. They had their backs to Ben. He slipped across the crowded restaurant back to where Chrissie waited.

"Chrissie, it's *Nick*! Remember how he used to say 'good as a juicy Georgia peach'? That other man asked him how he was doing, and he said it. Chrissie, it's him. Jan has spent all these years in the pen for nothing."

"We have to tell her so she can tell her lawyer!"

"Let's not say anything to anyone until we see Jan in two weeks."

They watched as Nick and his wife left the restaurant. He never saw them, and they waited awhile before leaving. They went to pay the check and asked the waitress, "Would you have any idea how long the Harpers have been married?"

"Oh, many years. They have three children who are grown and out on their own."

Ben and Chrissie ran to their car to head home. They didn't want anyone to see them.

"That scum! How could he do this horrible thing to Jan and ruin her life?"

They discussed this all the way home, promising each other not to say a word to anyone. For the next two weeks, they went to work, did their jobs, and tried to listen to anything they could, but no one was mentioning anything about Nick or Jan. It was as though they had forgotten the whole horrible ordeal.

Finally visiting day had arrived, the day to drive back to see Jan. They were excited to see her, and she was going to be shocked to hear about Nick. It took all day to drive to the institution. They decided not to stop in Cambridge anymore for fear of running into Nick.

As they sat in the waiting room to see Jan, they were laughing yet nervous about how to tell her about seeing Nick. She came in all smiles and happy to see her friends.

"Hey guys, my lawyer is going to court with the suit for the state to do my surgeries."

"Jan, we have something important to tell you. You are going to be shocked."

"Remember we told you about the new restaurant in Cambridge? Well, we stopped last time on our way home. You will never guess who we saw there."

"No, I wouldn't have any idea."

"Nick Reed! Only, his name is Thomas Harper, and there is a Mrs. Harper with three grown children."

"What? How do you know all this? It might not be him but maybe someone who looked like him."

"I followed him to the restroom. He was talking to another man, and he said, 'Good as a juicy Georgia peach.' I promise you, it was Nick!"

"That scum! He is part of this. He took everything away from me." Tears ran down Jan's face. Then she sat quietly. "Revenge is best served cold!"

"What do you mean?"

"Well, I am going to have a new face, a new body. I am going to ruin him and put him in here and take everything away from him."

"We are in, Jan! Whatever you have planned, we will help!"

"It won't be long until I get my new body, and then I am free. Then my new project will begin."

They had a nice visit the remainder of the day, and then Jan had to go back. As she was being escorted out, she said, "Remember, not a word to anyone." Jan was boiling inside; she was angry, so angry that now she wanted to kill him for all the damage he has caused her.

As she lay on her cot, all kinds of things went through her mind. She had to put together a plan, a no-fail plan to ruin him and take his life away from him. She slowly went to sleep, continuing to dream about her new life, which would come very soon.

Jan was very angry in the following days knowing she had been scammed and framed. She knew she had a chance to renew her life, and she was putting her ideas together to get back and put Nick in his place. As she thought about what had happened and how much she lost, the angrier she got. Now he needed to lose everything as well.

Ben and Chrissie had come to visit again.

"Guys, I am so glad to see you. We need to discuss the future. I need to know how deep you two are into putting Nick away."

"We are going all the way with you. We are very upset about this. He has it coming to him."

Jan proceeded to give instructions on her plans. "Anytime they ask you to work extra, do it. Get into every file, every design, everything you can get your hands on with his real name or with anything about the company being involved in anything. Make copies of all of it. Take it to my house and put everything in Dad's office."

"You got it. With the two of us, by the time you get out, we should have all the copies of everything in that building."

"It won't be long now until they start doing the surgeries. You can cut your visits down, especially if you can get overtime in to make copies of all the files."

During the rest of the visit, they discussed what they were going to do to bring this about. Laughing and joking with each other like old times, they could feel the love they shared for one another, and they knew their plan was going to be successful. At the end of the visit, Jan was escorted back to her cell.

Her meals were brought to her. When she had free time outside, she was escorted; they were not taking any chances of more problems or attacks. Jan felt safe and excited about the future. It helped the days to go by faster.

Jan's lawyer came to see her one afternoon. "We won, Jan! The state is going to bring a plastic surgeon in. You will be in the hospital ward under guards. It will probably take quite a while to get it all done, and then the healing process can really begin.

"Great! I need a new face and body so that when I get out, I can start a new life. Maybe even a new identity, yes, and a new name, that's what I need."

"We'll work on that when you are released. I probably won't be back for a while. I just need you to sign these papers for your surgery and the doctor."

Jan beamed from ear to ear. Things were falling into place, and she knew she was going to make it. She had more faith now than she had in a long time. She signed all the papers.

CHAPTER 13

It was time for her surgeries to begin. The doctor came to visit with Jan and discuss what they were going to do. Jan picked out things on her face for changes and pigmentation.

"I want to look totally different. I don't even want to look in any way how I did before all this happened."

"We can do it. I just need some measurements to prepare for the surgeries."

The very next day, Jan was transferred to the hospital ward. As she was putting her things up and getting settled in, she realized she was whistling and humming, not afraid or anxious in any way.

The next morning, the nurse came in and started preparations and gave Jan her preop shots to get her started on her first endeavor.

She became very sleepy and groggy. They wheeled her into the OR and then gave her the remaining shots. Jan could feel herself going out; the light turned to total darkness.

When she started to wake up, the nurse was talking to her. "You're going to feel some pain and be very groggy for a few days, so lie still."

She moaned the more she awoke, feeling the pain.

The doctor came in to check her over. He checked her real good. "I am changing some of the outer dressings. The nurse will be giving you pain medicine and antibiotics through the IV. You are doing just fine."

Jan felt so swollen that she didn't try to talk. She slept several days, barely knowing what was going on. The pain got less and less until she was awake.

After a week, the doctor arrived, and he checked Jan over and told her everything was doing just great. "Today, we are going to remove the bandages and let the healing take over. All the swelling should be gone."

He began cutting away the bandages and unwrapping it until it all lay on the floor. He handed her a mirror. She stared in the mirror. She didn't recognize the face looking back at her. She was beautiful. Her face was red and bruised, but the cuts and scars were all gone. Tears rolled down her face. She was so happy. She remembered she was happy with her looks before, but now she had a new start and a new body to go with it.

She continued to heal as one day led to another and one week led to two weeks. The doctor arrived, stating, "It's time to do your second surgery, and the nurse will prepare you."

The surgery went well. Jan woke up that evening sore and hurting. She knew it was for her own good, however. Each day the pain got less, and more and more dressings came off until finally she didn't need any bandages. She was back to normal to her waist. She looked great. She couldn't believe it how well it all came out. She was so proud. Now she looked even better than before the attack.

After a week, she was feeling great. The surgeon was ready to do another surgery. She continued to heal from the previous surgeries. Her spirit was healing, and she was getting stronger in every way. She was getting more and more used to the surgeries. She did her best to ignore the pain.

During the next month, she had three more surgeries. As she healed from each one, she was so thankful it was going so well. She didn't recognize the new person looking back at her, but she felt great. After the last surgery and all the bandages were removed, the doctor came in. "Well, we are done. Now it's all up to you. Make sure you eat well and healthy, drink a lot of water, and finish your vitamins and antibiotics, and you are as good as new!"

Within the next month, a therapist began to work with her to strengthen her muscles and get her toned up. Everything was good. She was walking better, and her voice was sounding better. She was so happy.

Ben and Chrissie came to see her. They didn't recognize her when she was escorted into the room.

"Well, what do you think?"

"No one will know you. That is such a good job, and you look absolutely great!"

"I am changing my name also. Do you guys have any ideas? Something unique and not expected, all to fit my new look as well."

"How about Karen?"

"Yeah, Karen DeAnn! Now a last name."

"How about Daniels?"

"Great! Karen DeAnn Daniels, I like it!"

"No one will even suspect it's me. A new person came in and bought my parents' house. I will have my lawyer change all the paperwork."

They visited the rest of the day and couldn't believe how strange it was to talk to a totally different person. They even noticed how her attitude and personality had changed. When visiting time was over, the guards came to escort her back to the hospital wing, and Ben and Chrissie left to make the long trip back home. They had taken a lot of overtime and had copied a lot of the files and had moved them to the house Jan would be moving into once she was released. They didn't know what she had planned, but step by step, it was going great.

Another month went by, and Jan's rehab was ending. She was healed; no scars and no areas showed from the attack. She looked for her lawyer so she could get things taken care of. To her surprise, he came to check on the results of her surgeries. Jan was escorted to the visiting room.

"Well, what do you think?"

"Jan? Is that you? What a great job!"

"I have also picked a new name: Karen DeAnn Daniels. I would like for you to do all the paperwork—birth certificate, social security, everything. Then change the name on my parents' house, where I will be living, and the bank accounts. Leave nothing to be questioned."

"I can do that. I came today to give you some more good news. There is a possibility for an early release!"

"Are you serious? You mean I don't have to do the last two years?"

"We will keep your release quiet, and I will have all your paperwork done to show a new person is moving into your parents' home. Should anyone check, Jan Reed will still be an inmate here."

"This is great! I can start my new life without anything hanging over my head."

No one anywhere knew the plans that Jan was coming up with—that is, except for Ben and Chrissie. Her lawyer was only trying to make the release and future easier for her.

As each day went by, she was super excited about what was taking place. Day after day, she kept preparing, doing her rehab and getting herself ready for the day she walked out.

Her lawyer put a For Sale sign on her parents' house—for show only, of course. That way, no questions would be asked. He then proceeded with all the paperwork and was very successful.

He prepared his motions for early release. He was aware that would take some time and prepared Jan for that. So he was surprised to be called after two weeks to give his presentation to the judge. No one could see why she shouldn't be released. After eight years, no one mentioned Nick Reed or the fire. The judge signed the release order. He immediately drove to the institution where Jan was. When she was escorted to the visiting room, she was shocked to see her lawyer there.

"Jan, you are released! I will be here next Monday to pick you up! I will have all your paperwork done, and you can walk out of here as Karen DeAnn Daniels, a new woman!"

The lawyer got busy and called Ben and Chrissie to help him prepare everything. Ben and Chrissie had cleaned up what they could from the fire and put everything in storage, and now they were going after a rental truck to move all her things home. They all agreed to meet at Jan's childhood home.

When they arrived, the attorney took down the For Sale sign. They unlocked the door and proceeded to go in and clean and scrub the house and unload and unpack all the belongings. The three continued nonstop and worked as long as they could. They accomplished a lot the first day, yet they had a long way to go, and then they had to get Jan picked up Monday morning. The three stayed at a hotel that night and were up early to get a long day in again.

Even though they had a lot of work to do, they all laughed and joked and had a great time. Jan was coming home! They were happy to make the preparations.

The cleaning was very successful, and they were down to the last of the boxes in the truck. They were pleased about finishing the job. Sunday evening, Jan's lawyer headed to pick up Jan. Ben and Chrissie stayed behind to make sure everything was unpacked and cleaned up. They were so excited about her return.

After driving all night and into the morning, Jan's lawyer had arrived to pick her up. She had gathered the few belongings she had and was escorted to the front of the institution to the release department. She was so happy to see her lawyer that she screeched with joy.

They walked out together to the car. Once in the car, he handed Jan her file. "You are now a free woman, Karen DeAnn Daniels!"

Tears rolled down her cheek. She had completed the first phase in her plans, and no one would ever know who she was.

It was a long drive, and the new Karen became very tired. As she closed her eyes, she could see her plans unfold. They pulled in the drive. She grabbed her things and ran to the house. Tears were flowing like rivers; everyone knew why she was crying.

"I don't know how I will get used to being here knowing I will never see my mom or dad here again."

"Just remember, now you are Karen DeAnn Daniels, and you are a private designer, and you can work right out of your own home."

She was so delighted.

Ben and Chrissie had quit their jobs to help with all the adjustments and to start her new company.

"It's going to take some time to get used to my new life. We will start by ordering and getting the equipment we need to get going. When I get more used to being Karen Daniels of Daniel's Designs, then I will get out in the area."

Ben nodded. "We need to get airtime on television and radio to get our company advertised and get the name out there."

"You take all the time you need. We can get things started, ordered, and in place. We can do any necessary legwork in the meantime."

"Oh, I am so glad you two are here with me. I am so afraid, but you two give me added strength."

The next day, they started getting the supplies that they needed in order. It was a very busy day. The evening came fast, the three happily fixing supper and discussing their progress and what needed to be done the next day and in the days to come. They finished eating and cleaned up the kitchen and retired to the living room to watch some television and enjoy the rest of the evening. The next morning came very early. They got breakfast out of the way. After cleaning the kitchen, they proceeded with the office work. The doorbell rang, catching them off guard a bit; however, it was a delivery truck, there to deliver equipment for the new office. They quickly got busy getting the drawing tables set up and copiers and file cabinets organized. They received the stationery, envelopes, office supplies, and equipment needed for the new business to run efficiently and get off the ground running. They booked airtime on the radio stations in the area and also set up airtime for television. Each day, more and more was accomplished. Soon the sign was placed in the front yard, making the business official. It took them about a week, and most of all the deeds were accomplished.

The second week came, and it looked as if things were starting to take off. The phones starting ringing, and clients set up appointments to meet and discuss jobs. Karen was becoming very at ease and comfortable in her new life. They had each consigned and contracted two clients within the first few weeks of being open. All three were busy working on the designs and new bids. Within a month's time, they had money coming into the business. New clients were coming in constantly to contract with the three.

Karen was feeling more comfortable and started leaving the house to go to sites and take measurements. Everyone who saw her was taken by her beauty and was happy to meet her. No one ever guessed they already knew her.

On weekends, Karen would go through the files from Brent and Nick to see if she could figure out why they ruined her life and caused the deaths of her parents. She prepared flyers and mailed them all over the state in hopes of getting closer to finding things out. She received more appointments from clients who wanted a change from Brent.

Daily, more business came to the office of Daniels Designs. All three were extremely happy, and more people were leaving her previous company. Karen got braver and started traveling out to see what she could find out. She continued to look through the files. There had to be a big reason why Brent was so threatened by her that they caused so much pain in her life, and she was serious about finding it all out.

"Well, my dear friends, what do you think of our business?"

"We never knew that it would turn out to be so good. We are all doing great. We are glad we left to come work for you!"

That weekend, as they were going through the files, Karen ran into something very suspicious. "You guys, come look at this. Here is a file on a Tina Sims. It is funny. I remember Nick talking about a design on property they were having trouble with."

"I remember doing a partial design on landscaping for a Tina Sims property, but I never heard where the property was."

"You know, I did a mall design on a Tina Sims project about four or five years ago, then all of a sudden Brent canceled the job," Ben blurted out.

"I think we found our ace, guys. Start looking in the computers and find and copy everything you find on Tina Sims from birth until now."

They worked the rest of the day to find out everything they could on Tina Sims's profile. It was getting late, and all were getting tired and hungry. "Okay, let's file everything in order and put it with the Tina Sims file, and when we get back to it, we'll pick up where we left off."

"Let's take a break and go out to eat for a change!" Ben suggested.

"Sounds good, let's go!" the girls agreed in unison.

Over dinner they discussed how close they were to finding out and discussed upcoming plans. They were so happy the business was going so well and they were going to solve the plot that caused Karen so many problems.

The remainder of the weekend, they relaxed and had fun; they did some shopping and had a lot of laughs. Monday morning came all too soon. It was business as usual. Phones were ringing off the hook, machines whirring; the office was abuzz with clients coming in for their scheduled appointments. Karen seemed very distracted. Her mind was going back and trying to remember what she could about the Tina Sims project. She just couldn't put it all together. The workweek was busy but went by very quickly. They completed a few jobs and were extremely happy. The clients were more than delighted with their work.

CHAPTER 14

On Saturday morning, after breakfast and when everything was cleaned up, they went to the office to continue their search on the Tina Sims project. They continued to make copies of everything they found. Lunchtime came. They took a fast sandwich break and were back at it. There were mountains of material they had copied. Then all of a sudden, everything stopped. It was as though Tina Sims had disappeared into thin air.

"I don't understand it, Karen. She just disappeared right before we were told to stop working on the projects. I bet that has something to do with it!"

"Check bank accounts, family, neighbors, medical records. We have to find her!"

There it was, a body was found north outside of Cambridge, a car in a canyon with a body found under the car.

"It was ruled an accident."

"Guess what?" popped up Ben. "She was seven months pregnant."

"Well, now I know how it is all tied together. I'm getting closer and closer to finding their dirty laundry. Is that all the information you can pull up? Let's quit for this weekend and pick up on it next weekend. We have a bunch of jobs to get finished this week. It is going to be hard for me to keep my mind on my work knowing we are getting closer."

"I know what you mean. We'll get it put together, and then we can go after Brent and Nick!"

"Let's go out tonight and eat. We can clean tomorrow and get ready for the week. We need a break tonight," Ben suggested.

The remainder of the weekend was busy. All three had their minds on what they had found out, and they knew they had to keep their heads to keep the business going.

Monday morning, they opened and, very soon, was busy with clients and their designs. They stayed busy all week and completed several small jobs. As more flyers were distributed, the more their business increased. When the days ended, they were exhausted but happy and successful.

Saturday came again, and as early as they could, they were back in the office.

"Okay, get the board over here. Let's do a time line and figure this out."

Once they got everything settled, Karen began, "Tina Sims was born in Leavenridge, where she grew up. When she was in high school, one night her parents were driving home, and they were run off the road and both killed by a drunk driver. She went to live with her mother's sister on a huge horse ranch in Craigmont. Her aunt's husband came up missing mysteriously. A year later, her aunt died from a massive heart attack. No one was left but Tina. She inherited everything, plus life insurance from all four. She continued to run the ranch, and then she met a man, Carl Reed. She fell in love and married him. She became pregnant, and then Carl was found dead from a mountain-climbing accident. When Tina was seven months along, she met Brent Wilson. She was also run off the road by a drunk driver. Brent Wilson inherited the ranch and all of her money."

Chrissie jumped in, "Well, folks, you have it. Look at the names Reed and Brent. Everyone is dead, and Brent got it all. It didn't work out right this time. There was a will, and they didn't get a dime. Jan may have died, but Karen arose out of those ashes."

They all laughed. Then Karen got serious. "We have them, and they are murdering people to get all their money. We have to find that property and get it bought up."

So they started looking for the property.

Ben jumped up. "I found it! It's twenty-five miles north of Craigmont. The foreman of the ranch is living there and caring for the horses. Get this, Brent Wilson is the owner!"

"I'm going there next week! Who knows, maybe I'll see Mr. Thomas Harper as well. It's time for me to start some pain of my own. Ben, when you get caught up, could you find the car that Tina was driving and also do some checking into the family background? We need to fill in the gaps and find out as much as we possibly can. Chrissie, we need to find out who burned up in my house and if Nick took out a life insurance policy. I don't see how he or Brent got a penny."

"Okay, will do!"

"Any questions about Jan Reed, she passed away from a violent beating and stabbing while she was doing her time in the penitentiary, got it?"

"Got it!"

The weekend zipped right along. Monday morning, Karen packed a small bag and said her good-byes to Ben and Chrissie. "I will call if there are any problems."

"Okay, if we don't hear from you, we will assume everything is going fine."

Karen got in her car and headed for Craigmont. It was a very long drive and took most of the day. When she arrived, it was dark, so she drove to a motel and checked in. She ordered room service and relaxed in front of the television. She grew very tired, so she showered and went to bed. Dozing off, she realized how important her friends were; she was already missing them.

She arose early, ordered breakfast, and got ready for her investigation. She drove to the vital statistics office, the morgue, and then to the doctor who took care of Tina. Then she went to find the ranch that once belonged to Tina. As she gathered her information, she decided to drive to Cambridge. She was becoming more informed about the past events. It was all coming together. She ordered breakfast as she got herself ready for another day.

She started out by checking newspaper articles on Thomas Harper—how long he had been married, his children, and any connection between him and Tina Sims. She drove to his house to see his lifestyle now. She did some shopping to make herself visible around town. Deciding then to have lunch back at the motel, she headed back. As she walked in, there he sat with the lovely Mrs. Harper. She sat across from the table on the other side of the room, hoping he would spot her. Sure enough, he did! He smiled her way occasionally. When she finished her meal, she got up and left. She continued driving about town, continuing to keep busy until dinnertime. She returned to the motel for dinner. She ordered and was writing some notes on things she wanted to check out when a shadow fell on her. She looked up, and there he stood as handsome as the first time she met him—Nick Reed. There he stood, her dead husband, the man who took everything good in her life away from her.

"Excuse me, is anyone joining you?"

"No, I am by myself."

"May I sit down?"

"Sure. Rest yourself and have some coffee."

"You're new in town? Do you work?"

"Yes, I own my own company, and I am here on a buying trip. I'll be going home tomorrow. My associates will be looking for me."

Her food was brought to her. She ate, listening to him. She was very nervous and also becoming angry with each word out of his mouth.

"What do you do for a living?"

"I'm an investor, and I buy rare items." As she finished her dinner, she had had all she could handle. "If you'll excuse me, I'm ready to retire for the night."

"How about a nightcap at the bar?"

"No, thank you. I don't drink, and as I said before, I am very tired."

"I'd like to walk you to your room."

"That won't be necessary. I am fine."

She paid her bill and went around the corner to watch if he was following her. She saw him come out and look around. He couldn't see her. He went to the desk to ask what room she was in. The desk manager replied, "I'm sorry, sir. I cannot give out any information about our guests." He turned around and left.

Karen saw him leave through the glass doors. She was glad to see him leave. She wanted no more to do or say to him. She returned to her room. She sat down to collect her notes and put them in order. She watched a little television then showered. She took some time to think about the last ten years and what had happened. As she crawled into bed, these thoughts continued to run across her mind.

Karen woke up early and ordered her breakfast and coffee in her room. When she finished, she packed up her things and got ready to check out. While checking out, she had her car brought to the front. The busboy loaded her bags, and she was on her way back home. She was glad to be leaving. She missed Ben and Chrissie and couldn't wait to tell them everything. The puzzle was finally fitting together, and she was pretty sure she knew what was going on.

Karen arrived home late, so she let herself in and went to her room to get ready for bed. She was so exhausted from the long trip. In the morning, she slipped her robe on and went to the kitchen. Ben and Chrissie had breakfast ready.

"We sure missed you! I hope you had a successful trip. We are starting to get backed up. I can't believe how our business has boomed."

The discussion soon turned to Karen's discoveries. "It looks like Brent met Tina and fell for her hard, then Nick met her and started dating her. Brent found out and went to Nick and threatened him to stop seeing her. Nick continued to see Tina on the sly. In the meantime, Brent had taken out a large insurance policy on Tina. He was also doing some forged designs on Tina's ranch. He had us all working on it. We have the forged files and contracts. That was all Nick's trips to South America, plus being Thomas Harper and being married. Brent forged a will to receive all of Tina's property and money. She never knew. Then three months later, Brent cut her brake line and drove behind her, shoving her in the canyon. Her car rolled on her after throwing her out, killing her and Nick's baby. Then Brent and Nick discussed this. Brent was threatening to tell Nick's wife. Nick couldn't afford this. He would lose everything, his wife and her money. Nick, being very angry, burned down Brent's home, killing his wife. Brent couldn't tell as all his plans would be in the tubes, and Nick couldn't report anything either. They both had everything to lose. They were afraid. With all of us working on the designs and contracts, we were too close, and Nick getting involved with me was the icing on the cake, so he had to get rid of me, our baby, and my parents. Now we get to start new problems in their lives!"

Ben popped up, "I found out some very interesting things as well. The body that was found in your house was the man that supposedly ran Tina off the road."

"Well now, how interesting. The loose ends are all tying up."

"Let's get enough evidence compiled together and send to the insurance company."

"Right now, we need to get to work. We sure don't want to lose any of our clients!"

The progress was very surprising, and everything was adding up. Now all they had to do was involve the right people, and Nick and Brent would be in the penitentiary for life and lose everything at the same time.

At the end of the day, they had gathered all the evidence and made copies, certifying them, including the autopsy report that showed that Tina had several barbiturates in her system. They made sure that nothing had their names anywhere. They put it all in the mail to the insurance company and the state attorney general.

"We will let that circulate awhile before going any further. It should keep them busy trying to figure out who's causing the problems."

As the days went by, the three got caught up taking care of clients and catching up on their work. They were at peace and happy to have figured out the mystery of what was going on.

Time swiftly passed by; soon a month had passed. One morning, as they ate breakfast, they decided to turn on the television. There it was, the answer to all their work! The attorney general was doing a deep and thorough investigation into forgeries from the Brent Design Company and the Gates Insurance Company for a forged insurance policy, and a false claim and also an investigation into the murder of Tina Sims.

The three jumped for joy. They were on their way. At least now it was all coming out in the open, and soon, they would pay for their crimes.

The three continued their work and their shared lives. They didn't need to do anything else yet. They wanted to see what would take place. Karen was mixing and visiting more with outside events and people she knew and was enjoying every minute. No one had any idea who she was. Her new life turned out to be very exciting, and she was progressing well. The Three Musketeers did everything together. They were happy, and they were glad to be together working and making a new life.

CHAPTER 15

About once a week, they heard on television that the investigation was in full swing, and a lot of other questions were coming up. They stated that there was another person possibly involved, a Cambridge man, none other than a man named Thomas Harper. It may also mean that there is a possibility of more deaths than just Tina Sims. The investigation would continue until the whole truth came out.

"Well, my friends, it's time to send another clue to the attorney general to keep the fire hot." They all laughed.

Karen found some of the articles and evidence to prove that both Brent and Thomas Harper were cheating on their wives with Tina and that Thomas was also the father of Tina's baby.

"That should keep their interests peaked and ready to dig deeper."

"They are going to be wondering where all this information is coming from."

"We will continue to keep a low profile. Maybe down the road they will want a witness to testify. I will be ready."

A week later, they announced on television they had received some very serious evidence, enough that arrests could be made, but at the time, they were questioning the two men.

Daniel's Design was picking up more and more business, a lot which came from Brent's. The word was, people were being laid off due to the investigation, and people were taking their business elsewhere.

The Real Estate and Investment Company, owned and operated by Thomas Harper, did not have any business going on either. It was like the two men had turned evil, and now they were going down.

The three kept up with the progress of the investigation through the television and newspapers. A few weeks later, they heard that Brent Designs was on the market as he had no business and the stigma was tearing the business up.

The insurance company was very close to making a decision, and it looked like he was going to have to pay back the life insurance on Tina Sims and charges would be brought up on him.

After another month, Karen sent copies of more evidence to bring Thomas Harper into the web. When checking on the television, it was announced how Mrs. Thomas Harper was filing for a divorce and charges were being brought up against Thomas Harper and Brent.

Everything was being taken away from them, just like how they'd taken everything from others. Both had been put under arrest and now were penniless. Things sure had taken a turn for the worse, and now it was time to turn the lights out permanently.

Karen gathered up the remaining evidence that Thomas Harper, aka Nick Reed, met and married Jan Reed and killed the man they hired to run Tina Sims off the road and burned his body in their house, framing Jan for Nick's murder and theft of designs. Jan lost her baby, was sent to the penitentiary for ten years, where she was brutally beaten and stabbed, all so Brent and Nick/Thomas could go on and continue to live their lie and keep all they stole. In the process, Nick/Thomas killed Brent's wife so neither one could report the other one without being convicted as well.

As soon as the attorney general received the remaining evidence, they started an in-depth investigation. Sure enough, the puzzle was now complete, and they were going to nail both men.

As the three were eating breakfast, they listened to the news report; a trial was soon to begin on this matter. The district attorney was seeking life. They continued to report on television about the trial. It was not looking good for Nick/Thomas and Brent. Karen felt sorry for them. They had to continue to kill, steal, and destroy to prove their purpose, to keep each other's silence, and to keep their lives as they knew it.

After a month of presenting the evidence, the jury was out for a very short time, and when they returned, they delivered a verdict of guilty. Sentencing would be in two weeks.

At the close of work, the Three Musketeers were exhausted. They went into the kitchen and started dinner. As they were preparing dinner, they decided to turn on the television to hear an update on the trial and found out both men were found guilty. They neither one had anything or anyone in their corner. They ruined many people's lives, but in the end they had nothing.

"Well, I am glad it's over. I am very sorry for them. I wonder if they feel it was all worth it."

"At least you now know why all this happened!"

"My parents paid the price with their lives, as did my baby!"

The room was quiet and filled with the sadness that remembering all the pain had brought.

They continued their days ahead a little happier and with the peace of freedom from the past problems. The design company was keeping them busy and keeping their minds off the trial. They had an idea what they would get when they were sentenced. They still wanted to hear it for their own peace of mind, however.

Karen kept up with the news while eating dinner. One night it was announced that the attorney general had received mountains of evidence from someone who was close to the case and had done a lot of investigation into the events. The attorney general was now looking for that person or persons.

"What do I do, guys? I don't want anyone to know who I really am. I want to remain Karen and forget the life I had as Jan. It's over. I died that night I was beaten and stabbed. The only ones who know are you two and my attorney." Karen was frantic.

"Hey, we have an idea. Brief us on everything—the whys and whos that we don't know. We'll contact the attorney general and say we sent the evidence. We have all the originals, and we knew Jan Reed, and we knew Ken and Corene Williams. We can do this!"

"I just don't know. I don't want Nick to know I'm still alive, and I hate asking you to lie for me."

Ben took her hand in his. "Let us do this. It will put an end to all of it. If we don't, they won't stop until they find you. This way, maybe they will be satisfied and drop it."

"Okay, let's try it." Karen started going through all the evidence with Ben and Chrissie, then they called the attorney general and spoke with the lead person available.

"I understand you are looking for the people who gave you the evidence for the arrests of Brent and Thomas Harper. I am that person, myself and a friend."

"We are going to need you to appear in court the day of the sentencing. Do we need to come get you and your friend, or can we count on you being there?"

"We will be there."

Ben and Chrissie spent the next week going over all the evidence to be prepared for the court date so that this long, drawn-out process could be put behind them.

The day before the sentencing day, Ben and Chrissie drove to Cambridge. They arrived late and found a room for the night. They ordered room service for dinner. They tried to make light of the situation by laughing and joking, also to calm their nerves.

"You know, Ben, I'm afraid. We have to get this right so they will leave Karen alone."

"I know. We will get it right, and everything will be okay now."

They watched some television to relax, and after a while, they decided they needed to go to bed. They had a long day ahead of them in court.

The next morning, they ordered breakfast, ate, and got ready for their day in court. As they pulled in the parking lot, they wished each other luck and reminded themselves to keep it real.

They were escorted to a waiting room until it was time for them to give their testimony. There was a speaker in the room. They could hear the preparations.

As the proceedings started, they heard the district attorney say, "We have located the people we received the evidence from to put this together. We would like their testimony on record to these charges." Chrissie was then called into the courtroom.

"Good morning, Miss Mahon! Did you volunteer to send evidence to the attorney general in this case?"

"Yes, I did."

"Why did you feel the need to investigate this case?"

"I worked for Mr. Brent at his design office. I was assigned to do designs on the Sims-Wilson project. After a month, when it was almost complete, it was canceled. That had never happened before. Then there were rumors the designs, and files were missing. A new face was about the building—a man, Nick Reed. He started dating a friend of ours, Jan Williams, one of the best designers we knew. One day I was in the file room, and I overheard some shouting. It was between Brent and Nick. Brent was upset about Nick dating Jan, especially after what had happened and what was going on. I became very suspicious of the events. However, Nick and Jan married. Eighteen months after their wedding, they were expecting a baby. Then Jan was framed for stealing the designs and contracts. When she returned home, her house burned down, and a body was found inside. They said it was Nick's. There was a trial. Jan was found guilty for conspiracy and murder and was sentenced to ten years. She lost her baby, and as her parents worked to prove her innocence, they also passed away. After eight years, Jan was severely beaten and stabbed. She was the most important thing in my life, and they took everything from her. So my friend Ben and I started looking at everything. On our way to visit Jan, we went a different route and stopped at a restaurant for dinner on our drive home. We saw Nick. We asked who he was, and the waitress told us it was Thomas Harper and his wife and that they had grown children. So then we went into all the files and found the lost files. We checked medical records, marital records, titles, deeds, insurance policies, etc. They didn't succeed in getting any money from Jan because when Jan was moved, her father left everything to Ben and me to take care of, including her life insurance. They got nothing! We pieced everything together and found that Brent was dating Tina and she was also seeing Nick. It upset Brent. He fed her pills and hired someone to run her off the road. She was pregnant with Nick's baby. Brent received everything Tina had by making a false will and false papers. Nick then killed Brent's wife so neither one could say anything because it would condemn both men. Then Nick met Jan and married her. They were expecting a baby. Brent and Nick killed the man that ran Tina off the road to use as Nick's body in the fire. The only reason Nick's wife was not killed was because she held all the money and Nick was to never inherit anything. It all goes to their children. Brent forged all the papers as Tina had no family. All the loose ends were taken care of."

"Well, I think that explains everything. Does anyone have any questions?"

"I feel Miss Mahon has explained everything quite well. Is there anything that Ben Peterson can tell us that we don't already know?" asked the judge.

"No, he assisted me in all my research and traveled with me to investigate this case as we knew our friend had no desire to steal or interfere in the records that Brent was holding but felt she was a threat for Nick."

"Thank you, Miss Mahon."

"Oh yes, one last question. Who is Karen DeAnn Daniels?"

"She is my new employer. I have quit Brent Designs, moved, and started a new job with a new design company, and I love it!"

"I am finished."

"Are there any more questions?"

"No."

"At this time, the defendants will rise. You two disgust me. You have killed and stolen to get through your everyday life making yourselves look like you are important. You have destroyed many families and many lives. I sentence both of you to finish your lives at the state pen with no possible chance of parole. May God have mercy on your souls."

It was over. Karen was safe, and Jan could stay buried. The judge added, "Everything you two own shall be sold, and the money will be returned to the people involved in this case. You two will now have a chance to feel what you put your victims through."

EPILOGUE

Ben and Chrissie left the courtroom smiling at each other. "We did it, Ben. Karen is safe. I can't wait to tell her everything will be okay."

"Just a minute, Ben and Chrissie!" They turned to see the attorney general. "Aren't you a bit curious why we didn't press the issue on Karen?"

"I guess we didn't think too much about it. I guess too nervous."

"After you called to confess you were the ones that sent in all the evidence, we investigated where Jan is, especially since the stabbing. We know she had several surgeries and changed all her existence to Karen DeAnn Daniels and that now she owns and operates Daniel's Designs."

"So what happens now? She only wants to stay out of existence. Her business is a success, and she wants to start a new, clean life as Karen, not Jan. That's why we did this—to protect her."

"It's all over now. They got what they deserved, and it's too bad that Jan spent eight long years in prison for nothing. It's so unjust. Tell her she's safe now. Her secret will remain safe. I'm the only one who knows who she is."

"Thank you so much. She will be happy to know."

Ben and Chrissie went back to the motel, ate an early dinner, and went to bed, so happy about the day's events. When morning came, they gathered their things, loaded the car, and headed home. It was a very long drive. When they arrived home, Karen was standing at the door.

"It's all over, Karen! The attorney general knows you are Jan and that you sent in the evidence. He said your secret is safe and you can remain Karen. They didn't push the issue in court."

"I guess Jan is really dead now, and we can leave her where she is. I am free at last. I can't believe it. I am free!"

"The judge gave Brent and Nick life without parole and took everything they owned, and all the people involved will get the liquidation of all assets."

"Maybe now Karen DeAnn Daniels will have a better life than Jan Williams Reed."

ABOUT THE AUTHOR

RHONDA RUSSELL is married and currently lives in Lubbock, Texas. She is a retired licensed vocational nurse; she loves caring for people and animals. She is the mother of three beautiful grown daughters and grandmother to nine active grandchildren. She is also a pet parent, having rescued six Chihuahuas, one white dove, and five cats. Rhonda's faith runs deep; she is an avid follower of God.